The Eagle of the Ninth

Rosemary Sutcliff

The Eagle of the Ninth

Adapted by
Rosemary Wagner

Oxford University Press

Oxford University Press, Walton Street, Oxford OX2 6DP
Oxford London Glasgow New York Toronto
Melbourne Wellington Kuala Lumpur Singapore Jakarta
Hong Kong Tokyo Delhi Bombay Calcutta Madras
Karachi Nairobi Dar es Salaam Cape Town

ISBN 0 19 424206 4

The Eagle of the Ninth
1000 headword level

Set, printed and bound in Great Britain by
Cox & Wyman Ltd, Reading
Typeset in Linotype Garamond

I

The road was rough now as they marched west to Isca Dumnoniorum. It's an old British way, Marcus thought. Wider than it was, perhaps, but little better.

One two, one two, one two, came the heavy sound of the cohort's feet behind him.

There were many other travellers on the road today. But at the sight of the Standard they quickly got themselves and their animals out of the soldiers' way.

One two, one two, one two.

The Cohort Commander held his head high. This was his first Command, and it was with a new cohort. The six hundred yellow-haired men behind him were all from Gaul, but he himself was Roman.

Centurion Marcus Flavius Aquila was as thin and dark as the Gauls were broad and fair. His dark-skinned face was strong and hard, but full of laughter lines.

He was remembering his past now, as they marched through this new and wild country. It's strange to think I've only been with the Eagles for a year! he thought. I was glad to leave my aunt's house in Rome, I must say. And that stupid fat penpusher, her husband. He knew nothing of a soldier's life!

He thought even further back and remembered sadly his family farm at Clusium. He had a quiet and happy life as a child, living there with his mother. And his father, the soldier, who was nearly always away – in Judaea, Egypt, and then in Britain. Marcus remembered how wonderful it was when he came home!

But then one day his father's Legion, the Ninth Spanish marched into North Britain and never came back. Not long after that Marcus's mother died, and Marcus had to go to Rome.

As the evening light fell like gold on the Isca Dumnoniorum

Road, he thought of his father. The small, dark man who taught him to hunt and fish, and always seemed to be laughing. Marcus remembered that last time he came home, when he himself was only ten years old.

His father's eyes were brighter than ever. He was going to command the first cohort of the Spanish Legion. He would take care of the Eagle and be second-in-command of the Legion itself. He was like a happy boy about it.

But Marcus' mother looked worried. 'If it was any *other* Legion . . .' she said. 'You told me yourself that the Spanish has a bad name.'

But her husband just laughed and turned to Marcus. 'Soon it will be your turn,' he said. And the light caught in the green stone of the ring he always wore. 'It has seen bad times, but we will make a Legion of the Spanish yet, you and I.'

(One two, one two, one two, went the feet.)

And now it is my turn, thought Marcus. Here I am in Britain, a Commander myself now. Perhaps I shall be able to find out something about my father's lost legion.

They marched over a hill and suddenly Isca Dumnoniorum lay before them. The fortress on the Red Mountain was dark with shadows against the evening sky. Blue wood-smoke rose from the British town below it.

The road led straight through the town and up the hill beyond to the fort. Marcus took a good look at the British as he passed by. The men in their red and yellow cloaks watched the soldiers with cold eyes. The women sat at work in hut doorways, with very white arms. Dogs and other animals ran in and out of the huts. There was a strong smell of horse.

One day there will be straight streets here, Marcus thought. The Roman way of life will win. But as yet it's a place where two worlds meet. He looked up at the fort. So, he thought, this is where I'll spend the next year!

'You have brought clear skies with you,' Centurion Quintus Hilarion said, looking out of the window of the Commander's rooms. 'But don't think it will last.'

6

'Is it as bad as that?' Centurion Marcus Aquila asked. He was sitting on the table.

'Quite as bad as that! It rains all the time here in the west. One year is enough in a place like this, I can tell you.'

He turned from the window. 'It's so lonely, too. I like to have my friends around me.' He smiled. 'Ah well, it's all right for me. I am off to Durinum as soon as I have marched my men back to Isca.'

'Is Durinum your home?' Marcus asked.

'Yes. My father lives there now. It's a good enough place. And where will you go when you have time off? I suppose you have no one out here to go to, as you have just come from home.'

'I have an uncle at Calleva,' Marcus said. 'But I have never yet met him. And I have no one at home.'

'Father and mother both dead?' Hilarion asked with friendly interest.

'Yes. My father went with the Ninth Legion.'

'That is bad.' Hilarion shook his head. 'There are a lot of ugly stories about them. Of course they did lose the Eagle.'

'Since not one man of the Legion came back, it is no wonder that the Eagle did not either,' Marcus answered hotly.

'Of course not,' Hilarion agreed with a smile. 'Don't worry, Marcus, I didn't mean it was your father's fault.'

Marcus smiled back at him. He looked around the rooms. Soon they would be his. Through an opening he could see a small room. It contained a bed with brightly-coloured British covers.

'I wonder,' Marcus said, 'what does one do here? Is there good hunting?'

'Good enough. There are plenty of wolves in the winter and the forest is full of animals. There are some hunters below in the town. They will take you out for the price of the day's work. It's not safe to go alone of course.'

Marcus agreed. 'Is there anything else I should know? I am new to this country.'

The other thought for a moment. 'Well, yes there is. You need to watch out for the Druids. If one of them appears in these parts, be prepared.'

7

'The Druids?' Marcus was surprised. 'But I thought Suetonius Paulinus killed them all sixty years ago.'

Hilarion shook his head. 'They still show themselves from time to time. And when they do there is usually trouble for the Eagles. They can make the people do anything in the name of their gods.'

Hilarion stood up. 'Come,' he said, 'It will be best to do the late rounds together tonight.' He reached for his sword.

There came the sound of footsteps; a red light shone at the window. They went out together to see the men keep watch.

After tonight I'll do this alone, Marcus thought.

The next morning Hilarion and his men marched out of the fortress. At their head was the gold and red Cohort Standard. Marcus stood and watched it till it disappeared into the bright sunlight. Then the heavy sound of marching feet could be heard no more.

Marcus was alone with his first command.

2

Before many days were over Marcus felt completely at home in the fort. Roman fortresses were all built to the same plan. Inside the British fort the soldiers lived in much the same way as they did in Rome or Egypt.

It took a little longer to get to know his men. All five centurions were much older than Marcus. It was not easy to give them orders they did not like – after all, I've only been with the Eagles a year, Marcus thought. But he managed it. Galba and Paulus showed anger at first, but there was soon a good understanding between them and the Cohort Commander.

Centurion Drusillus was Marcus's second-in-Command. They got on well from the start, and Marcus liked him very much. Drusillus was able to tell Marcus a lot of useful things. Marcus needed his help quite often that summer. It was hard work in those early days, and he was glad to have Drusillus behind him. But he loved the work, and was happy.

And it was not all work. Some days he took off to go hunting, and the hunting was good. The Briton he took with him was called Cradoc. Not much older than Marcus, Cradoc was a hunter and horseman.

One late summer morning, Marcus went down to the British town from the fort, carrying his hunting spears. It was very early, and the sun was not yet up. Usually he loved this time: the cool morning air, and the smells rising from the wet earth and trees. But today he was a little worried. Not much, but enough to spoil his enjoyment.

The men were saying there was a Druid somewhere around. Marcus remembered Hilarion's words. Still, it's probably nothing to worry about, he thought. But I'll keep my eyes and ears open, all the same. And as the corn is bad again this year, there could be trouble.

He reached the group of huts that belonged to Cradoc. A girl with a baby came to the doorway. She was tall, as most British women were, and carried herself like a queen. But Marcus noticed a strange look on her face: the look of someone with a secret.

'My man is out behind with his chariot team. If the Commander goes to look he will find him,' she said, and stepped back into the hut.

Marcus went to look. Cradoc wished him good day in the Celtic language, and Marcus replied in the same. He spoke it easily now. But he was looking past Cradoc to the horses. 'So you drive chariot teams of four here?' he asked in surprise.

'We have learned some lessons from Rome,' Cradoc answered. 'Have you not seen my team before?'

Marcus shook his head. 'I did not even know you were a charioteer. Of course I should have realized. The British are all charioteers.'

'The Commander is wrong,' Cradoc said, touching the shining neck of one of the horses. 'The British can all drive a little. But not everyone is a charioteer.'

'*You* are a charioteer?'

9

'They say I am among the best of my people,' Cradoc answered quietly.

'May I see your team?' Marcus asked.

The other stood to one side for him without a word. The four beautiful black animals came to Marcus almost like dogs. They are smaller than the Arab team I drove in Rome, he thought, and more heavily built. But how gentle and alive they seem! He turned from one to the other and ran his hand over their bodies.

'Will you let me try them?' Marcus turned back to Cradoc, his eyes bright. Oh, I want to be out in the wind again, he was thinking, to feel the chariot floor shaking below me, and those lovely animals racing at my command!

'I will not sell them.'

'I don't want to buy them. I just want to try them.'

'The Commander is also a charioteer?' Cradoc asked.

'They say I am the best in my Legion,' Marcus said.

'But still, these black jewels of mine are not easy,' Cradoc said.

'Well, let's see,' Marcus said, smiling. 'If I cannot manage them well enough to please you, over ground that you choose, I will give you this.' He pointed to the red jewel that held his cloak. 'If I can, I'll take one of your hunting spears. Or anything else that you name.'

Cradoc gave Marcus a long cool look. Then he said, 'Very well.'

'When shall I try them?' Marcus asked.

'I have to take some horses to Durinum tomorrow; but in eight days I shall be back. We will give you a try then. And now it is time for us to go.'

'Agreed,' Marcus said. He left the four black horses with a last look, then followed Cradoc out. They called the dogs, picked up their hunting-spears, and disappeared into the wild countryside.

Cradoc was away longer than he thought. There was little corn, and it was all in from the fields by the time he returned. It will be a hungry winter, Marcus thought, as he went to meet Cradoc for the charioteering match.

The other man was already waiting near the river. As soon as he saw Marcus he jumped into the chariot, turned the team, and raced towards him through the long grass. The sun shone on the metal on Cradoc's body and the horses' heads; the charioteer's long hair flew out behind him.

Marcus stood his ground, but not without some fear. At the last moment Cradoc stopped the horses almost on top of him.

'Very clever,' Marcus said with a smile. Then he jumped in beside Cradoc. He took up the driver's place and Cradoc stepped back.

'Take them across to that dead tree over there, to begin with,' Cradoc said.

'Soon,' Marcus said. 'I am not yet ready.'

This chariot was twice as big as the Roman racing chariots. They only had room for the driver. Marcus wanted to get used to the different feel of this one. He set his feet wide apart and started the team, gently at first, then faster. Just before the tree he turned them, as Cradoc ordered. Then he took the team quickly in and out of a line of sticks, touching none of them. Then he let the horses race at full speed to the edge of the wood.

It was like being born over again! The cool wind on his face was like water, singing past his ears. Marcus called out to the horses in the Celtic language, pushing them on. 'On, brave hearts! On, beautiful ones! Faster, faster!' The dark forest edge raced by the grass disappeared under the wheels. He and his team were one – a star shooting down the sky; a flying ball of speed. . . .

Then at a word from Cradoc he stopped the team. Cradoc jumped down and went to the horses' heads.

'Well?' Marcus asked. His face was wet.

Cradoc looked up, without a smile. 'The Commander begins to be a charioteer,' he said.

'I have not driven a better team than these,' Marcus said. 'Do I win my spear?'

'Come and choose it for yourself,' said the other. 'Few people could manage this team better than you.'

They drove back slowly, walking the horses through the summer evening.

Soon afterwards Marcus walked back to the fort. He carried his new spear. Children and dogs were playing together in the low sunshine. It all seemed very peaceful, yet he felt worried. He remembered the look in the girl Guinhumara's eyes. It was still there when he chose the spear. And among the spears there was that war-spear. 'It was my father's,' Cradoc said. 'It was in his hand when he died. See, his blood is still on it.'

But it was in excellent condition, Marcus thought now, clean and bright with new colours – why? And in how many other huts was there a war-spear like this?

He entered the fort deep in thought.

3

Two nights later a centurion woke Marcus from his sleep.

'What is it, Centurion?'

'The soldiers on the south wall report sounds of movement between us and the town, sir.'

Marcus was out of bed at once. He reached for his heavy cloak.

'Can they see anything?'

'No, sir, but they are sure something is moving down there.'

They were out in the dark now, climbing the steps to the wall. The shape of a soldier rose up before them. Marcus went to the look-out. Low cloud covered the sky and the stars. A light rain was falling. All below was black. He could hear nothing.

He waited; suddenly there came the cry of a hunting night-bird, followed by a deep silence. At last Marcus thought he heard a movement. But it was gone before he could be sure. Then the sound came again, and this time dark shapes moved suddenly below them.

The centurion laughed. 'Someone will be busy tomorrow looking for the cows he's lost!'

Lost cows! So that was all. But Marcus was not so sure. He

remembered that war-spear of Cradoc's. 'They could use the cows as cover,' he said. 'Centurion, this is my first command: if I am being a fool, *that* must excuse me. I am going back to get some more clothes on. Get the cohort out to action stations as quietly as possible.'

It did not take him long to put on his battle-clothes. As he returned he saw his men running out into the dark.. Centurion Drusillus was waiting for him. 'I think I've gone mad, Centurion,' he said to the older man.

'No, you are right,' Drusillus answered. 'It does not pay to take chances in these parts – and there was a new moon last night.'

Marcus understood what he meant. In his world the gods showed themselves in new moons. An attack was quite possible at the new moon. He turned to one side to give an order. Then they waited in silence. Marcus' hands were wet, his mouth dry.

The attack came. Silent shadows rose from all sides, racing forward. Then the soldiers rose as one man to meet them: the time for silence was past. The men shouted at the tops of their voices as they fought the British back from the walls.

It was light by the time the attack was over. Marcus looked at his second-in-command. 'How long can we hold out?' he asked softly.

'For a few days, with luck,' Drusillus answered.

'We could get more men from Durinum in three, perhaps two days,' Marcus said, 'but will they see our sign?'

'The cloud is too low at present,' said Drusillus, looking at the sky. 'And it's too wet. They will not see the smoke.'

'We'll just have to wait then,' said Marcus. He managed to keep the worry out of his face, as he went down among the men. 'Well done, boys!' he shouted with a laugh, 'We'll have some food before they come on again!'

Marcus himself had no time to eat. He had too many other things to do and think about. There was Centurion Galba, for one. He was out in the country with a Century of men. He was coming back at midday. How could Marcus get them all safely back into the fort?

He gave orders for a fire to be lit on the roof. That would give them a sign that something was wrong. Then he asked Lutorius to keep watch for them.

The next attack came in full daylight. The British broke suddenly from cover, shouting wildly. They made for the fortress doors this time, using fallen trees to try to break them down. They held torches of fire above their heads and their swords and war-spears shone red in the light.

The Romans shot arrow after arrow at them, but nothing seemed to stop them. They pushed on, even over their dead. Marcus noticed a Druid in the middle of them, a wild man with long hair and white clothes.

'Shoot that madman for me,' Marcus said quietly to the soldier beside him. The man shot, but missed the Druid.

At last the British fell back.

Once more the fort had a breathing space. They counted the men dead or hurt -- there were more than forty.

Marcus looked up at the sky. Still the same low cloud and light rain. He went up to the roof.

'It's no use, sir,' said the soldier who sat by the fire.

Marcus shook his head. Suddenly he found himself calling on the gods for help. 'Great God Mithras,' he said under his breath, 'King of the Skies, free us from these rains and clouds. Send your light upon us, and hear our cry!'

He turned back to the soldier. 'All we can do is wait,' he said, 'be ready to make the fire smoke at any moment.'

Some time later, as he was talking to Drusillus, Marcus looked over the walls. 'Do you see what I see?' he asked suddenly. 'I think the hills are growing clearer!'

It was so. Little by little the light grew. The rain lifted. At once the soldier sent up the smoke, and Marcus watched and waited for an answer. At last it came. A day's march to the east, a dark line of smoke rose into the air.

The call for help was seen. In two or three days more men would be here. Every man in the fort at once felt better.

Only an hour later Galba's men were seen on their way back to the fort. Marcus ran at once to look.

'The British have broken cover, sir,' Centurion Drusillus said.

'I can see them,' Marcus said. 'Right. I need half a Century of men.' He began to take off his cloak.

The centurion gave the order and turned back to him. 'You'd better let me take them, sir.'

Marcus shook his head. 'This is for me,' he said. He walked quickly over to the men at the wooden gates, and stood at their head. 'Open up!' he ordered. 'Now!'

The gates opened wide. Marcus and his men raced out in a close group like some great animal; they threw themselves upon the surprised British.

'Out, swords!' cried Marcus as they began to fight.

'Caesar! Caesar!' the men shouted.

Behind them soldiers on horseback kept the way to the fort clear. In front Galba and his men came fighting forward to join them. But between them, the shouting British fought strongly. Marcus saw the Druid among them. He laughed and ran forward.

Galba and his men joined them at last. At once the Romans began to fall back, slowly towards the fortress gate.

Back, and back. Nearly there! thought Marcus, catching sight of the wall out of the corner of his eye.

But suddenly the crowd around him was growing thinner. Why? And here came his answer. Chariots! War-chariots with sharp knives on their wheels were racing down towards them from the edge of the woods.

The Romans turned and ran, as one man, for the fort. But Marcus knew they could not reach it in time. What could he do?

He stopped, turned and stood full in the way of the chariots. He decided to jump for the charioteer. If he brought him down the whole team would lose its direction. It was a small chance but he had to take it. It might give his men just enough time to save their lives. For Marcus himself it was death. He was quite clear about that.

They were right upon him. The noise of the horses seemed to fill the world. They were the same black horses he called his brothers only two days ago. Marcus looked up and saw the grey face of Cradoc, the charioteer. For a second their eyes met. Two men who might have been friends. Then Marcus jumped in under the other man's spear. He pulled hard at Cradoc. The men went down together. There was a terrible sound of crashing wood and horses. Then sky and earth changed places. Marcus fell under the wheels and darkness closed over him.

4

His leg hurt terribly. It was all he could think of as the darkness slowly left him. People moved near him and hands touched him. But everything was like a dream. Nothing was real but the fire in his leg.

Then one morning Marcus opened his eyes and knew where he was: on his back in his own bed in his own room. He could just see a square of blue sky through the window.

So he was not dead after all. He was a little surprised but not very interested. He was not dead but he was hurt. His leg still felt very bad. But he was alive! Marcus remembered the battle now. It all seemed very long ago. He was not too worried about it. From the sounds outside he could tell the fort was still safely in Roman hands.

Someone came in. Marcus turned his head slowly – it seemed very heavy. It was the fortress's doctor. His eyes were red: he looked tired.

'Ah, Aulus,' Marcus said. 'You haven't been to bed for a month, I think.'

'Not quite so long as that,' the doctor said. He came forward quickly to look at Marcus. 'Good. Very good,' he said.

'How long?' Macrus asked.

'Six days; yes, yes, or perhaps seven.'

Suddenly everything seemed near and important again. 'The force from Durinum? Did the men get through to us then?'

'Yes, yes,' Aulus answered. 'Most of a cohort of the Legion from Durinum.'

'I must see Centurion Drusillus – and the Commander of the men from Durinum.'

'Soon perhaps, if you lie still,' Aulus said.

'No, not soon, now! Aulus, it is an order; I am still in command of this—' He tried to sit up, but fell back at once with a cry.

'There, now you have made it worse!' said Aulus. 'You must lie still as I tell you. Now, drink this.' He gave Marcus a drink. It tasted strange, and at once he fell asleep again.

Centurion Drusillus came next day and told Marcus about all the happenings since the battle. Marcus listened very carefully. He found it hard to do so at first. But he still had questions for the other man.

'Drusillus, what happened to the Druid?'

'Gone to meet his own gods, sir.'

'And the charioteer – my charioteer?'

'Dead,' said Drusillus, 'and we thought you were too.'

After a moment's silence Marcus asked, 'Who brought me in?'

'Many of us together – it was all so quick – Galba turned back to you and we brought out more men.'

'Were they not all cut to pieces by the chariots?' Marcus asked quickly.

'Not too badly. You stopped most of the chariots by your brave action. Galba is hurt but not dangerously.'

'Tell him I shall come and visit him if I am on my feet before him,' Marcus said. 'And tell the men I always *have* said the Fourth Gaulish was the finest cohort with the Eagles.'

'I will, sir,' Drusillus said. 'They have all been very worried about you.' He got up, smiling, and left.

Marcus lay back and thought over it all. He remembered Cradoc and felt sad. I liked that man, he thought, yet he led the attack! But he was driven by his gods, I suppose. He had to do it. And now he is dead and the little British town burned to the ground.

Later the Commander of the force from Durinum came to see him. Marcus did not like him. Centurion Maximus was a fine

17

soldier but a cold man. He stood in the doorway and told Marcus that everything was in order again.

'I shall continue my march north tomorrow,' he said coolly. 'I shall leave two Centuries to bring the fort up to its usual numbers and Centurion Herpinius will take command until the new Commander arrives from Isca.'

What he said was very reasonable, Marcus realized. But it was the way he said it that he did not like. Also Marcus was beginning to feel afraid. A new Commander! he thought. But I will be well again soon, won't I?

Day followed day. Marcus still had no interest in food, but thought his leg was getting better. And then they told him.

'You'll never be able to fight with the Eagles again,' Aulus said sadly. 'But just you wait, that leg will carry you well enough one day. But not for a long time. No, I don't know how long.'

Marcus took it very quietly, but inside he felt terrible. So, he thought, I'm going to lose everything I care about. Life with the Eagles is the only kind of life I've ever wanted. The only kind of life I know. And now it's over, I'll never be Prefect of an Egyptian Legion; I'll never be able to buy back my father's farm in the Etruscan hills. I've lost the Legion. I've lost my land. What sort of future can I hope for now?

A few days later Marcus heard the sounds of the new Commander arriving. Soon he will have these rooms, he thought unhappily. As soon as I am well enough to travel. So I am to go to Uncle Aquila. My father's brother. It will be interesting to meet him for the first time. I wonder if he is like my father?

There were quick footsteps outside his window. A moment later the new Commander stood in the doorway. It was the owner of the chariot team Marcus drove in Rome.

'Cassius!' Marcus smiled.

'My dear Marcus!' Cassius came over to his bedside. 'How is your leg?'

'It is getting better, slowly.'

'Good, I am glad of that.'

'What soldiers have you brought with you?'

'Two Centuries of the Third. They are Gaul's like the rest. Good fellows – but your men have given them a lot to live up to.'

'I don't think there'll be any more trouble in these parts,' Marcus said. 'Centurion Maximus took good care of that.' He looked unhappy.

'Ah, you mean the burned villages? I can see you did not like Centurion Maximus.'

'I did not.'

'Perhaps if you saw the report he sent in when he got back, you'd feel more friendly towards him.'

'It was good?' asked Marcus, surprised.

'Very,' Cassius answered. 'I think they will soon add some Golden Leaves to the Standard of the Gaulish Fourth, as a mark of its success.'

There was a short silence. Then Marcus said, 'Good. The men have truly won the mark. It will be their first. I am pleased it was under my command. Send me word if it does happen.'

'I will,' Cassius said. 'And now I must go to the bath-house. I am dusty from head to foot.' He stopped a moment, looking down at Marcus. 'Don't worry. I'll look after your cohort well.'

Marcus laughed, but his heart was sad. 'I should think so. They are a fine cohort – the best with the Legion; and – good luck to you with them!'

5

By the end of October, Marcus was living in the house of his Uncle Aquila at Calleva. The fort was now seven days' march away.

It was not a good time for Marcus. His leg still hurt badly, and he was very lonely. He spent most of his days alone in the long room in the centre of the house. Uncle Aquila looked in on him from time to time but he was usually too busy writing a book in his study.

Stephanos, his uncle's old Greek body-slave looked after Marcus now as well as his master. The only other person around was Sasticca, the housekeeper. She was a tall, strong old woman who never left Marcus alone. She kept on bringing him food – he was too thin, she said. But Marcus became quite angry with her. He did not want people to be kind to him just then.

He was very sad to be away from the Legions, and also his own land. Here in Britain it was cold and wet: wild weather day after day. He needed young company but there was no one of his own age. Even the dog Procyon had grey hairs on his nose.

But one good thing happened, not long after he came to Calleva. Cassius wrote to say that the Gaulish Fourth was going to receive the Golden Leaves. And later Marcus himself received the Gold Ring of the Eagles – to his great surprise. From that day onwards it never left his finger.

The days grew shorter and the nights longer. On the twenty-fourth of December, Marcus and his uncle sat by a wood fire after their evening meal. Uncle Aquila was a big man. He was not at all like Marcus's father.

Marcus looked over at his uncle. 'Ulpius was here this morning,' he said.

'Ah, our fat doctor. Did he say anything interesting?'

'Only the usual things. That I must wait and wait!' Marcus laughed, but there was a sad note in his voice. 'He called me his dear young man! Fat! He is an ugly old man.'

'So,' Uncle Aquila agreed. 'Still, you *must* wait, there's nothing else for it!'

'But that's the trouble,' Marcus said. 'How long can I wait?'

Uncle Aquila looked at him with a question in his eyes.

'I've been here two months now and we've never spoken of the future. But we must talk about it some time.'

'Some time, yes, but not now. No need to trouble about the future until that leg will carry you.'

'But the gods only know how long that will be. Do you not see, sir, I cannot stay with you for ever!'

'Oh, my good fellow, do try not to be such a fool!' cried Uncle Aquila. His voice was angry but his eyes were kind. 'I am not a rich man. But neither am I too poor to offer my own brother's son a roof over his head. You do not get in my way. To tell the truth I forget you are here most of the time. Of course you will stay here, unless—' he stopped for a moment. 'Would you rather go home?'

'Home?' Marcus repeated.

'Yes, I suppose you still have a home with that fool, my sister?'

'And Uncle Tullus Lepidus?' Marcus shook his head violently. 'Oh no thank you. That's no place for me!'

'Well, it's best for you to stay then,' his uncle said.

The two men fell silent. The wind shook the house. Marcus thought of life in the fortress on this cold winter night. He thought back to a year ago, at Isca, when all was new to him. And when I had everything before me, he thought unhappily. To shut out these dark thoughts he looked up.

'Why did you stay here in Britain, Uncle Aquila? Why didn't you go back home?'

'I had nothing to take me back,' he answered. 'I spent most of my years with the Eagles here. I have made friends here – a few. The only woman I ever cared for lies at Glevum.'

'I never knew—' said Marcus. 'What was she like?'

'Very pretty. She was the daughter of my old Commander. She had a lot of soft brown hair. Eighteen when she died. I was twenty-two.'

Marcus said nothing. There seemed nothing to say. But Uncle Aquila saw the look on his face and laughed. 'No, you have it all quite wrong. I am quite happy with things as they are.'

'I think I understand,' Marcus said. They fell silent again.

Then Uncle Aquila looked up with a smile. 'Well, well, all this talk of the past, it won't do. It's time we had a little fun, you and I.'

'All right. What shall we do?' Marcus returned the smile.

'I think we'll go to see the Winter Games tomorrow. Wild animals, gladiators, that sort of thing. Not quite up to what you see in Rome, but good enough for us. Yes, we'll go there.'

And they went. Slaves carried Marcus on a bed. 'I feel like a fine lady,' he said, looking uncomfortable. They arrived early. It was cold, but the air smelled good to Marcus. I've been inside too long, he thought. He pulled his cloak close round him and watched the other people taking their seats.

The British may not like many of the Roman ways, he thought, but they have certainly taken to the Games. They were coming in in crowds. One British family came and sat near Marcus and his uncle. The man and woman looked rich, and were dressed in Roman clothes. They had a young girl with them, of perhaps twelve or thirteen. Her face seemed all golden eyes in the shadow of her dark cloak. The man and Uncle Aquila spoke to each other.

'Who are they?' Marcus asked Uncle Aquila under his breath.

'They are our next-door neighbours,' he answered. 'Kaeso and his wife Valaria.'

'Are they? But the little girl? She is not their daughter, is she?'

But he got no answer to this question. At that moment the music sounded and the Games began. The double doors at the far side of the ring opened, and a line of gladiators marched out. The crowd shouted wildly at them.

They look quite good, Marcus thought. Too good, maybe, though probably they are all slaves. Oh dear, I hate all this. Men should not fight each other to the death just to amuse a crowd.

The men stopped for a moment before them. Marcus caught the eyes of one of them. He was rather short for a Briton, but powerful. On his ear was the mark of a slave. The look in his wide grey eyes made Marcus go cold. That man is afraid, he thought, afraid – afraid. The fear went through Marcus himself.

But before the gladiators, came the animal fights. Two wolves and a lion were driven into the ring. The lion did not want to fight for some reason. Soon it was killed, to great shouts from the crowd. Marcus looked across at the girl in the dark cloak. Her eyes were wide with fear; her face white. Why on earth do they bring a little thing like her to such rough Games as these, he thought angrily.

And so it went on. The blood lay thick on the ring floor. Between the fights men came with sand to cover it.

At last two gladiators stepped out from the double doors. The crowd fell silent. Here was the real thing: a fight to the death.

Marcus recognized the man with the sword: it was the slave with the fear in his eyes. The other man, with a spear, was small and dark. He looked like a Greek.

The fight seemed to go on for hours. Marcus held his breath. But in the end the Greek had the other man at his feet and held his spear over him. The crowd shouted for his blood.

Marcus stood up, forgetting his leg. He caught the eyes of the slave once again. Marcus turned to the crowd and made the 'thumbs up' sign. Let the man live! it said, and Marcus's eyes were bright and questioning. Please! he cried inside. How can you want him to die. Thumbs up! Thumbs up, you fools! He felt as if he himself was in the fight.

Uncle Aquila's thumb was also up. At last Marcus saw a few more, then more. Then as thumb after thumb went up the Greek put down his spear and stepped back.

Marcus took a deep breath, and fell back into his seat. Suddenly he noticed his leg again. It was hurting badly.

That evening Marcus asked his uncle: 'What will become of that fellow now.'

'The young fool with the sword? They'll sell him, certainly. The crowd won't want to see him fight again.'

'That's what I thought,' Marcus said. 'So I've decided to buy him.'

Uncle Aquila looked at him in surprise.

'I have enough money left from my pay,' Marcus went on, 'and there's not much to spend it on here. Would you have him under your roof?'

'I suppose so,' said Uncle Aquila, 'though I don't understand what you need a gladiator for.'

Marcus laughed. 'I don't want a gladiator. I need a body-slave. I can't go on asking so much of your Stephanos.'

'And what makes you think that a gladiator will make a good body-slave?'

'I don't know if he will,' Marcus said, 'I just want to buy him.'

'Very well, then,' Uncle Aquila said. 'But don't offer too much for him. And sleep with a knife by your bed ever after.'

6

'Centurion Marcus, I have brought the new slave.'

It was the following evening. Marcus looked up. Stephanos stood in the doorway. The new slave came forward, and Stephanos stepped back into the night. For a long moment the two young men looked at each other.

'So it is you,' the slave said at last.

'Yes, it is I.'

The silence began again and again the slave broke it.

'Why did you turn the crowd's feeling yesterday? I did not ask for help.'

'Perhaps that was why.'

'I was afraid yesterday. I, who have been a fighting man.'

'I know,' Marcus said, 'but still you did not ask for your life.'

'Why have you bought me?'

'I need a body-slave.'

'It is unusual to choose a gladiator.'

'I wanted an unusual body-slave,' Marcus smiled. 'Not like Stephanos. He's been a slave all his life and so is — nothing more.'

It was a strange way for master and slave to talk.

'I have only been a slave for two years,' said the other quietly.

'And before that you were a fighter — and your name?'

'I am Esca, son of Cunoval, of the Brigantes people.'

'And I am — I was a centurion with the Second Legion,' Marcus said. Roman and Briton looked across at each other.

'I know,' Esca said. 'Stephanos told me. And also that my Master has a bad leg. I am sorry for that.'

'Thank you,' said Marcus.

'I chose not to escape,' Esca said, looking down, 'on my way here. I could have done so easily. But I thought perhaps it was

24

you we were going to.' He brought out a thin knife from under his clothes. 'I had this.'

'And now?' Marcus said.

Esca let the knife fall on to the table at Marcus's side. 'I am the centurion's dog,' he said. 'I will lie at the centurion's feet.'

So Esca became Marcus's slave. He carried a spear and stood behind Marcus's place at meals. He did everything for his master and slept across his door at night. He made a very good body-slave and Marcus was well pleased.

The weeks went by and suddenly there was a promise of spring in the air. Marcus's leg was slowly getting better. He could move around the house more and more easily now. As time passed he left his stick behind and walked with a hand on Esca's arm instead. It seemed natural to do that. He did not realize it, but he was becoming more of a friend than a master to Esca. But Esca never forgot that he was a slave.

That winter there was a lot of trouble with wolves. They were so hungry they came out of the woods and hunted under the walls of Calleva. One day Esca returned from the town with news of a wolf-hunt.

'It is going to take place tomorrow,' he said. 'Isn't it exciting? Everyone is going to take part in the sport — some Roman soldiers as well. He told Marcus all about it.

Marcus wished he could go too. But it seemed unlikely that he would ever hunt again. 'Esca,' he said suddenly, 'you must go on this wolf-hunt. You must, I say so.'

Esca's face broke into a happy smile. 'Oh but I can't leave you for a night, and perhaps also a day.'

'I shall manage well enough with Stephanos,' Marcus answered. 'Now what will you do for spears?'

In the dark of that night Marcus heard Esca get up softly. 'Are you going now?' he called.

'Yes, if the centurion is still sure — quite sure?'

'Of course I am. Go and get your wolf.'

'I wish you were coming too,' Esca said quickly.

'Perhaps another year,' Marcus said. 'Good hunting, Esca.'

Esca returned in the grey light of early morning next day.

'Esca – how did it go?'

'The hunting was good,' Esca said. He came over to Marcus's bed. He was carrying something in his arm under his rough cloak. 'I have brought back the fruits of my hunting for the centurion,' he said, and set the thing down. It was alive and gave a little cry at being moved. Marcus put out his hand. It was warm.

'Esca! A new-born wolf?' he said, feeling its little head.

Esca brought a light. Marcus saw that he was right. The little animal shut its eyes against the yellow light.

'My people sometimes take the young ones when a she-wolf is killed,' Esca said. 'They can learn to run with the dogs.'

'Is he hungry?' Marcus asked.

'No. See, he is half asleep already; that's why he's so gentle.'

'How did you get him?'

'We killed a she-wolf, so I and two others went to look for the young ones. They killed the rest, those fools of the South, but I saved this one. His father came. They are good fathers, the wolf kind. It was a fight. Yes! a good fight.'

'But you put yourself in great danger,' Marcus said. 'You should not have done so, Esca!'

Esca spoke coldly. 'I forgot you own my body, sir,' he said in a hard voice.

'Don't be a fool!' Marcus said quickly. 'I didn't mean that, and you know it.'

There was a long silence. The two young men looked at each other and there was no laughter now in their faces.

'Esca,' Marcus said at last. 'What has happened?'

'Nothing.'

'That's not true,' Marcus said. 'Esca, I want an answer.'

The other moved a little. then he said at last. 'There was a young soldier, Placidus his name was. He followed us, and watched me kill the wolf. He saw me cleaning my spear and laughed. "That was well done," he said. Then he noticed the mark on my ear. "For a slave," he said. I was very angry. "Your master has paid good money for your body," he went on, "he will not thank you if you get killed. Remember that next time you want to hunt a wolf." '

Marcus felt cold with anger against the soldier. Quickly he reached out his free hand and took the other man by the arm. 'Esca, you don't believe that I think of you as that young soldier does?'

Esca shook his head. 'No sir, you are not like Placidus,' he said. 'You are not unkind to your dog.'

'Oh Esca!' Marcus cried out. 'Don't talk to me of dogs. Have I not shown you clearly enough all this time? I do not think of you as a slave! To me you are as any other man, and I talk to you as such. You don't do the same with me. Why not? And now—'

Marcus moved suddenly, then cried out, 'And now he's bitten me! The little wolf you gave me! Mithras! His mouth is full of knives!'

'Then you must pay me for them,' said Esca. The two men began to laugh and the bad feeling was forgotten.

The other people in the house soon got used to the little wolf. Stephanos did not like the idea of a wolf in the house, but Sasticca was pleased for Marcus. Uncle Aquila was too deep in his books to notice. The dog Procyon was afraid at first, but soon forgot he was not a dog.

Life went on as usual, but Marcus and Esca were growing closer. One day when they were in the bath-house they heard the noise of a chariot racing in the street outside.

'It's not often we hear that sound,' Marcus said.

'It's Lucius Urbanus,' said Esca. 'Oh, listen to him. He's not good enough to drive horses.'

Marcus pulled on his clothes. 'So you also are a charioteer,' he said.

'I was my father's charioteer,' Esca said. 'But that was a long time ago.'

Marcus sat down. 'Esca, how did you come to be a gladiator, then?'

Esca stood silent for a moment, then sat down also. 'My father was the leader of our people. We love to be free, and one day we rose up against the Legions. We fought hard but lost. There were few of us left and they sold us as slaves.'

'And the rest of your family?' Marcus asked after a moment.

'My father and two brothers died,' Esca said. 'My mother also. My father killed her before the Romans broke through. She wished it so.'

There was a long silence and then Marcus said softly, 'Mithras! What a story!'

'It is not unusual,' Esca said. He began to tell Marcus about the old times. 'I remember as a child,' he went on, 'I once saw a Legion marching north. It never came marching back. I remember the Eagle. It shone, golden in the sun. Then it disappeared in the cloud over the mountains. There were strange stories about that Legion.'

'Yes, I've heard those stories,' Marcus said. 'Esca, that was my father's Legion.'

7

Two steps led down from Uncle Aquila's house into the garden. It was rather a wild garden. But to Marcus, who had been inside all winter, it seemed a wonderfully wide and shining place. Now he was well enough to come outside he spent many happy hours here. Between the wild fruit-trees he could look across British Calleva to the forest country. It went on for mile after mile, blue and far away.

Now, in the early spring, the birds were singing. Marcus sat in the sun and worked on some wood. He enjoyed using his hands. Cub, the young wolf, lay close beside him, a little ball at his feet.

And then he saw that he was no longer alone with Cub. A girl was standing among the wild fruit-trees. A British girl in a light yellow dress. She was holding back her heavy red-gold hair with one hand.

They looked at each other in silence for a moment. Then the girl said, 'I have waited a long time for you to look up.'

'I'm sorry,' Marcus said, 'I was busy with this woodwork.'

She came a step nearer. May I see the little wolf? I have never seen one before.'

And Marcus smiled suddenly. 'Of course. Here he is.' He reached down and set Cub on his feet. He kept his hand under his small body. 'Be careful. He is not used to strangers.'

The girl gave him a smile and bent down, holding out her hands slowly to Cub. The little animal began to smell at her fingers. 'What is his name?' she asked.

'Just Cub.'

'Cub,' she said gently, 'Cub.' He moved towards her. 'See, we are friends, you and I.'

She was about thirteen, Marcus thought. A tall thin girl with a face that went down to a sharp point. Have I seen her somewhere before? he wondered.

'How did you know about Cub?' he asked at last.

She looked up. 'Narcissa, my slave, told me, about a month ago. At first I did not believe her. But then I heard one of your slaves call to another. "Your master's wolf has bitten me!" so I knew it was true.'

Marcus laughed, and so did the girl. Her teeth were as white and sharp as Cub's. Now Marcus remembered. Of course!

'I saw you at the Winter Games,' he said. 'But your hair was hidden under your cloak. That's why I did not remember you at first.'

'But I remember you!' said the girl. 'Nissa says you bought that gladiator. I am glad.'

'You did not like the Games, did you?' Marcus asked.

She shook her head. 'No, it is not right. Animals – and people – should be free.'

A cool wind blew across the garden. Marcus looked at the girl in her thin dress.

'You are cold,' he said, and reached for his old soldier's cloak. 'Put this on.'

29

'Don't you want it?'

'No, I have thicker clothes than you. So. Now come and sit here next to me.'

She did so at once, pulling the cloak around her. 'This is a centurion's cloak,' she said.

'I am Marcus Aquila. Once I was Cohort Centurion with the Second Legion.'

The girl looked at him in silence for a moment. Then she said, 'I know. Does your leg hurt you still?'

'Sometimes,' Marcus said. 'Did Nissa tell you that too?'

'Yes.'

'And what is your name?'

'My aunt and uncle call me Camilla but my real name is Cottia,' the girl said. 'They like everything to be very Roman, you see.'

'And you do not?' he said.

'I? I am of the Iceni people! So is my Aunt Valaria, though she likes to forget it.'

'I once knew a black chariot team who came from the Iceni,' Marcus said.

'Did you? Were they yours?' Her face was bright with interest.

Marcus shook his head. 'They weren't mine. I only drove them once. It was wonderful.'

'We all love horses, we of the Iceni,' said Cottia. Her voice became sad. 'My father was killed, breaking a young horse. That's why I live with Aunt Valaria now.'

'I am sorry. And your mother?'

'She is well, I suppose. She went to live with a hunter and there was no room in his house for me. So my mother gave me to Aunt Valaria. She has no children of her own.'

'Poor Cottia,' Marcus said softly.

'Oh no. I did not want to live in that hunter's house. He was not *my* father. But I do hate living with my aunt. I hate living in a town full of straight lines, and being shut up indoors, and being called Camilla. They want me to be a Roman girl and I won't!'

Marcus smiled. 'There doesn't seem to be much danger of that.'

'No. I will not let them. At night I lie in bed and think – and think about my home, the birds and the horses—' she broke off. 'But we are talking in my language now!'

She pulled the cloak more closely round her. 'I like being inside your cloak,' she said happily. 'I feel warm and safe – like a bird.'

There came the sound of a high voice from the next-door garden. 'Camilla! My Lady Camilla!'

Cottia shook her head. 'That's Nissa. I must go.' She got up slowly. 'Let me come again! Please let me.'

'Come when it pleases you,' Marcus said quickly. 'I shall be glad to see you.'

'I shall come tomorrow,' Cottia told him, and left, carrying herself like a queen. Marcus thought of Guinhumara. Most British women seem to carry themselves like that, he thought. I wonder what happened to Guinhumara and her baby.

Later he spoke with Esca. 'Esca, why do the British hate us so much?' he asked.

'We have ways of our own,' said Esca.

'But Rome has good things to offer you. We can make good roads, buildings—'

'Straight roads are not enough,' said Esca. 'The price is too high. Your lives are full of order. We do not understand that. We like to be free, like water in a river, to go where we want when we want. We do not understand your world of stone walls and straight lines.'

Yes, the two worlds are very different, Marcus thought. And yet people like us can forget all that and still be friends – Esca, Cottia, and me.

8

Cottia did not come the next day. Marcus kept looking for her, then said to himself, well, why should she come?

Then on the third day he heard her call his name. He looked up. There she was again, among the wild fruit-trees.

'Marcus! Marcus!' she began. 'They say I must not come again.'

Marcus put down the spear he was cleaning. 'Why?'

'Aunt Valaria says that Roman girls do not do as I have done. But I'm not a Roman girl; and oh, Marcus, you must make her let me come! You *must*!'

'She *shall* let you come,' Marcus said quickly. 'But it may take time. Now go, before they catch you.'

She disappeared. Marcus suddenly felt happy again.

That evening he asked Uncle Aquila to talk to the Lady Valaria.

'But I don't really know the woman. Why do you want the girl to come?'

'Oh – because she and Cub understand each other.'

'I don't know,' Uncle Aquila shook his head. 'It was peaceful in this house before you came.' He smiled. 'But I suppose you must have your own way.'

Marcus never knew how Uncle Aquila managed it. But from that time on Cottia came and went as it pleased her. And it pleased Marcus.

Marcus was happy in her company. They laughed a lot, played games and talked for hours. Marcus told Cottia long stories about his old home in the Etruscan hills. It seemed to bring it all back – the birds, the sun, the farmhouse, his mother at the door at the end of the day, and the smell of supper. And Cottia never grew tired of hearing the stories.

But towards the end of the summer Marcus began to have

more and more trouble with his leg. He tried to forget about it. But it was clearly getting worse.

One hot evening as Marcus and Uncle Aquila sat together, Uncle Aquila noticed that Marcus kept moving his leg.

'Is your leg hurting badly tonight?' he asked.

'No, sir. Why?' Marcus said.

'Oh, I just wondered. You are quite sure?'

'Quite.'

Uncle Aquila looked him in the face. 'Come, Marcus, don't try to hide things from me. I know that's not true. Your leg is worse. I've been watching you and I can see how much it hurts you. So I'm going to do something about it. Ulpius clearly doesn't know his job. I'll call in Rufrius Galarius from Durinum. He knows what's what. He is an old friend of mine.'

Rufrius Galarius came a few days later. He felt Marcus's leg with very sure and gentle hands. At last he looked up. 'Who on earth cleaned up this leg?' he asked, with anger in his voice.

'The fortress's doctor at Isca Dumnoniorum,' Marcus said.

Galarius shook his head.' He's been there twenty years and is drunk half the time, I'm sure of that.' He sat down on the edge of the bed. 'The thing is – he didn't finish his work,' he said.

Marcus went cold. 'You mean – it has to be done again?'

'Yes,' Galarius answered. 'You will have no peace until it is opened up and cleaned again.'

'When—' Marcus began.

'In the morning.' He put a hand on Marcus's arm. 'As soon as possible.'

Marcus lay still and tried to smile. 'I think I am – rather tired,' he said weakly.

'Soon you will be better,' Galarius said. 'I promise you that.' He stayed on a little while at Marcus's side and talked to him. When the doctor left, Marcus realized just how afraid he was. His whole body was shaking. He felt cold and very alone.

But soon Cub came to him and pushed his head under Marcus's arm.

'Thanks, Cub,' he said, holding him close.

Then Esca came. The two men were talking when suddenly they heard the high voice of a girl. 'Let me pass. If you don't, I'll bite!' There was the sound of fighting, followed by a shout from Stephanos. Then Cottia ran into the room, her hair like gold around her face.

Marcus sat up. 'Cottia! What have you done to Stephanos?'

'I bit his hand,' she answered. 'He tried to keep me out.'

'But what are you doing here, my Lady?'

She came close. 'Why didn't you tell me?' she asked.

'Tell you what?' But he knew what.

'About the Knife-Doctor. I saw him come and Nissa told me why.'

'Nissa talks too much,' Marcus said. 'I did not want you to know until it was all over.'

Her eyes were wide with fear. 'What will he do to you?'

He told her.

'I shall wait at the bottom of the garden tomorrow morning,' Cottia said. 'I shall wait for Esca to come and tell me when it's all over. If anyone tries to take me away I shall bite them. You will send Esca, won't you?'

Marcus agreed. 'Very well. Esca shall come and tell you.'

There was a long silence. Then Cottia said. 'I wish it could be me instead.'

Marcus was touched. 'Thank you, Cottia. I shall remember that. And now you must go home.'

She left without another word. And Marcus no longer felt so alone.

Rufrius Galarius came very early the next morning. Marcus was already awake. Esca brought in hot water and Galarius opened his case. 'Now,' he said at last, turning to Marcus, 'if you are ready?'

'Quite ready,' Marcus said. He shut his eyes hard so as not to see.

A long while later he awoke from the darkness. For a moment he thought it was Aulus standing beside him, as it was a year ago. Then he saw Esca standing behind Galarius, and Uncle Aquila in the doorway.

His leg hurt very much, but in a different way now. 'Oh!' Marcus cried out as he tried to move.

The doctor put out his hand. 'Yes, it will seem sharp at first,' he agreed, 'but it will get less, soon.'

Marcus looked up into his face. 'Have you finished?' he asked.

'I have,' Galarius answered. There was blood on his hand. 'In a few months' time you will be well again. Lie still and rest now. I will come back again this evening.'

Then Marcus found Esca beside him, holding a cup. 'Cottia – and Cub,' he tried to say.

'I will see to them soon, but first you must drink this.'

He drank, and looked into Esca's face. It was grey.

'Was it as bad as that?' he asked, trying to laugh.

Esca smiled. 'Go to sleep.'

9

It was eight months later. A Roman and a Briton stood on a hillside, a mile or two south of Calleva. Between them was a young wolf. The Roman had his hand on its neck.

Suddenly Marcus let go of the wolf. 'Go free, brother,' he said softly to Cub. 'Off you go now. Good hunting.' Cub looked up in surprise. Then his nose caught the smell of the woods. He was gone in a moment, deep into the forest.

Marcus turned to Esca. 'It had to be,' he said sadly. 'We have to give him the chance to be free.'

'He will come back to you, you will see,' said Esca. 'He knows the way home.'

They walked back slowly. Marcus's leg was well now. It would never be straight again and he would not be able to return to the Legions. But he was strong again and glad of that.

But what was he going to do with himself and his life now? The question worried Marcus more and more. He had no money to start a farm. I'll have to be someone's secretary, he thought unhappily. I'll talk to Uncle Aquila about it tonight.

Then he remembered. Uncle Aquila's old friend, the Legate of the Sixth Legion was coming tonight.

Oh well, it can wait another day, Marcus thought. After all, my present way of life's not so bad. Now he could get about again, he and Esca had plenty of fun. They spent much time in Calleva and often went riding in the country. He was seeing less of Cottia than he used to, he realized. But I never forget her, he thought. I would not like to lose her.

There were two strangers in the long room with Uncle Aquila when they entered. One was the Legate, the other a young soldier.

'Ah, you are back, Marcus,' said Uncle Aquila. 'Claudius, this is my brother's son, Marcus. Marcus, this is my very old friend, Claudius Hieronimianus, Legate of the Sixth Legion.'

The young soldier, it seemed, was called Placidus. Where have I heard that name before? Marcus asked himself. The two older men left Marcus and Placidus together. Marcus found the young soldier difficult to talk to. He seemed to have no interest in anything. Marcus did not like him at all.

Suddenly Placidus jumped. 'In the name of all the gods! A wolf!' he cried.

Marcus turned. There in the doorway stood Cub.

'Cub!' Marcus called. 'Cub!' The animal raced forward and into his arms. Marcus laughed with happiness and caught the great head in his hands. 'So you have come back, brother,' he said. 'You have come back, Cub!'

'It is a wolf! It really *is* a wolf – though it acts like a young dog!' said Placidus. 'How long have you had him?'

'Since he was very small, more than a year ago,' Marcus said.

'Then if I am not mistaken I saw him taken in the woods after his mother was killed. A wild young Briton brought him out – said he was slave to a Marcus Aquila. I remember now.'

'You are not mistaken,' Marcus said quietly. 'The wild young Briton told me that story.'

At that moment Stephanos entered and said that dinner was ready. Just in time, thought Marcus. I could get quite angry with this Placidus fellow.

They ate very well that evening. We should have a Legate to stay more often, Marcus thought, as they all lay back after the meal.

The talk turned to Eburacum. 'I must come up and visit the place,' Uncle Aquila said. 'I haven't been there for 25 years.'

'Yes, you must do that,' the Legate said, as he set down his cup. 'Come up some time after I return.'

'You wouldn't recognize the Station now,' said Placidus. 'A man could almost live there. It's not as it was in the time of the Spanish Legion.'

The Legate looked into his cup thoughtfully. 'I don't know,' he said. 'Sometimes I feel that the past lives on at Eburacum.'

Marcus turned on him quickly. 'You mean, sir?'

'The Ninth Legion left their mark on Eburacum. You still see British women whose children have Spanish faces. And the Spanish gods are not forgotten. It's all there still; a new Legion has come, but people don't forget.' He shook his head. 'There is something strange about the place.' He gave a short laugh. 'Even I sometimes look up to the mountains and wait for the lost Legion to come marching home.'

There was a long silence. A cold wind seemed to blow through the room.

Then Marcus said, 'Have you any idea what became of the Spanish Legion, sir?'

The Legate looked at him closely. 'Why, is it important to you?'

'Yes. My father was their First Cohort Commander – Uncle Aquila's brother.'

The Legate turned his head. 'Aquila, I never knew that.'

'Oh yes,' said Uncle Aquila. 'Perhaps I never spoke of him to you. We never saw much of each other. There were twenty years between us.'

'I see,' said the Legate. He turned back to Marcus. 'Possibly they were cut off somewhere and completely destroyed. No man was left to carry back word of it.'

'Oh, but could that really happen, sir?' Placidus put in. 'Four thousand men destroyed and no one hears of it? No, I think that they grew tired of life with the Eagles. The men killed their leaders and ran away to start new lives with the Britons.'

Marcus said nothing, but his mouth shut into a hard, hot line.

'No, I don't think that is very probable,' said the Legate.

'No, perhaps not, sir.' Placidus answered in his soft voice. 'Of course I only thought that because of the stories people tell about the Spanish Legion. They are not usually good stories.'

'But you do not really think they were all destroyed either, do you, sir?' Marcus helped himself to fruit he did not want.

'I don't like to believe it, no,' said the Legate. 'Could any Roman Legion fall so low? No, there has been some different talk, lately, along the Wall. People are saying that the Spanish Legion did go down fighting. The Eagle has been seen. The Northern peoples have set it up as a sort of god, they say.'

'What does that mean?' Marcus asked.

'Well, a Legion doing as Placidus says – running away – giving up – would probably hide the Eagle. Or throw it into the nearest river. Something like that. But an Eagle taken in war is very different. To the Painted People it must seem like the god of the Legion. So they make much of it. Set it up as a god to make the young men strong in war and help the corn grow. Do you see now?'

Marcus saw. 'What are you going to do about it, sir?' he asked, after a moment.

'Nothing. The story may not be true.'

'But if it is?'

'There's still nothing I can do about it.'

'But sir, it's the Eagle! The Spanish Legion's lost Eagle!' Marcus almost shouted.

'Eagle lost – everything lost,' said the Legate. 'Oh yes, I know.'

'More than that, sir,' Marcus's eyes shone. 'If the Eagle is found – and brought back, the Legion can be formed again.'

'I know,' said the Legate. 'And there's something else which interests me even more. If trouble breaks out again in the north, the Painted People will use the Roman Eagle against us. It will make them feel strong. But I still can't take any action. If I send in men it will mean open war. A whole Legion would find it hard to win through and there are only three in Britain.'

'But where a Legion cannot get through, one man might; at least to find out if it's true about the Eagle.'

'I agree, if the right man came forward. He would have to know the people of the north and be accepted by them. He would have to care very deeply about the Spanish Legion's Eagle.' He put down his cup. 'If I had such a one among my young men, I would give him his marching orders. The matter seems important enough for that.'

'Send me,' said Marcus. He looked at each of the faces round the table; then he turned to the entrance and called, 'Esca! Esca!'

'Now by the—' began Uncle Aquila and stopped. For once he could find nothing to say.

No one else spoke.

Esca appeared. 'The centurion called?'

Marcus told him his plan in a few words. 'You will come with me, Esca?'

Esca moved forward to his master's side. His eyes were very bright. 'I will come,' he said.

Marcus turned back to the Legate. 'Esca was born and grew up where the Wall runs now. The Eagle was my father's. We are the men you need. Send us.'

The silence ended suddenly as Uncle Aquila crashed his hand on the table. 'This is madness! Complete madness!'

'No sir, it's not!' said Marcus. 'I have a good plan. It will work. In the name of Light, listen to me.'

Uncle Aquila opened his mouth to answer but the Legate said quietly, 'Let the boy speak, Aquila.'

Marcus took a deep breath, then began to speak.

'Claudius Hieronimianus, you say the man must be accepted in the north, so that the people let him pass. What about a travelling eye-doctor? There are many bad eyes here in the north. Half the travellers on the road are eye-doctors. Rufrius Galarius told me of such a man. He even went as far as Ireland and returned safely.' He looked hard at the two older men. 'We may not be able to bring back the Eagle. But we shall at least find out if the story is true.'

There was a long silence. Uncle Aquila broke it. 'A clever plan, I'm sure. But you've forgotten one thing.'

'What's that?'

'You know nothing about the work of an eye-doctor.'

'That's true of most "eye-doctors" already on the roads. But I shall go on a visit to Rufrius Galarius. He will know enough about it to give me some medicines and tell me how to use them.'

Then the Legate asked, 'But how will you manage with that leg of yours?'

'It's almost as good as it used to be,' Marcus answered. 'If we have to run for it, it will not make things easier, of course. But in strange country we won't have a dog's chance on the run anyway.'

Again there was silence. Marcus watched their faces. They were trying to work out his chances, he could see. The matter became more and more important to him with every passing moment. I must go, he thought, it will mean the life or death of my father's Legion.

'Claudius Hieronimianus,' he said at last, 'do I get my marching orders?'

His uncle answered first. 'If one of my family wishes to break his neck in a clean cause, I shall not stop him,' he said.

The Legate said, 'Do you really understand what you'll go into? Valentia is no longer held by us. You will go out alone into enemy land. If you run into trouble, Rome can do nothing to help you.'

'I understand that,' Marcus said. 'But I shall not be alone. Esca goes with me.'

Claudius Hieronimianus bent his head. 'Go then. I am not your Legate, but I give you your marching orders.'

Later Placidus said a most surprising thing. 'I almost wish there was room for a third on this mad journey. I should like to come with you.'

For a moment Marcus almost liked him. But that feeling did not last long. For then Placidus said, 'Are you sure you'll be safe with that wild Briton of yours?'

'Esca?' Marcus said in surprise. 'Yes, quite sure.'

'You know best, I suppose,' said the other. 'But I should not like my life to rest in the hands of a slave.'

'Esca and I—' Marcus began hotly, then broke off. 'Esca has been with me a long time. He did everything for me when I was sick with this leg.'

'Why not? He is your slave,' Placidus said coolly.

This took Marcus by surprise. He no longer thought of Esca as a slave. 'That was not his reason,' he said. 'It is not the reason he comes with me now.'

'Is it not? Oh, Marcus, you've not lived. Slaves are all – slaves. Give him the chance to be free and see what happens.'

'I will,' Marcus said. 'Thanks, Placidus, I will!'

When Marcus entered his bedroom that night, Esca was waiting for him. 'When do we start?' he asked.

Marcus closed the door and stood with his back against it. 'The morning after next, probably – but that can wait. First you must take this,' he held out a piece of paper.

Esca took it in surprise and held it up to the light. Then he shook his head. 'I can't read it,' he said. 'What is it?'

'It says you are a free man, Esca,' Marcus said. 'I made it out this evening.'

Esca looked down at it once more, then said, 'I am free? Free to go?'

'Yes,' Marcus said. 'Free to go, Esca.'

There was a long silence. Then Esca said, 'Are you sending me away?'

'No! You may go or stay as you wish.'

Esca smiled. 'Then I will stay,' he said.

'Good!' said Marcus. 'And will you still come with me, but as my friend?' He looked into Esca's face.

'Of course,' answered the other. 'But I have always been your friend.'

On their last evening Marcus spoke to Cottia. He told her the whole story. Her face grew sad. 'But why don't they send someone else for this Eagle, if they want it so much?' she cried. 'Why do *you* need to go?'

41

'It was my father's Eagle,' Marcus told her.

'It is for him that you are doing it?'

'Among other things, yes,' Marcus said.

'I don't think I quite understand,' Cottia said, 'but I see you must go. When will you start?'

'Tomorrow morning. I shall go down to Rufrius Galarius first.'

'And when will you come back?'

'I don't know. Maybe, if all goes well, before winter.'

'And Esca goes with you. And Cub?'

'Esca,' Marcus said. 'Not Cub. I leave Cub to you. You must come and see him every day and talk to him about me. That way neither of you will forget me.'

'I won't forget you, Marcus,' Cottia said softly.

'Good. Oh, and Cottia – tell no one about the Eagle. It must stay a secret.'

Her smile came but was gone in a moment. 'Yes, Marcus.'

'Now I must go, Cottia. But there's one more thing I'd like you to do for me. Will you look after this while I am away?' He pulled the Gold Ring of the Eagles off his finger. 'I cannot wear it where I am going. Will you keep it safe for me until I come back?'

'Yes, Marcus.' Her fingers closed over it. He tried to think of something to say, but he could not find the right words. She looked so young and alone.

'You must go now,' he said. 'The Light of the Sun be with you, Cottia.'

'And with you,' said Cottia. 'And with you, Marcus. I shall wait for you.'

Then she turned and disappeared through the wild fruit-trees.

10

The great Wall of Hadrian ran from Luguvallium in the west to Segedunum in the east. Eighty miles of fortresses, castles and new stone-work shut out the Painted People of the north.

On a morning in early summer two travellers arrived at the fortress of Chilurnium. They asked to pass through to the north. They were riding horses which used to belong to the Legions, and wore British clothes. Esca wore the clothes of his own people, and looked much as usual, but dirtier. Marcus looked very different. Now his face and neck were dark with hair; he wore a bright red hat on the back of his head.

A long full cloak covered British dress of yellow and purple. He looked dirty. There was no longer anything about him of a Centurion of the Eagle. He looked much like any other travelling eye-doctor, except for his age. He was a little too young. On his box of medicines was written the name 'Demetrius of Alexandria, Eye-Doctor.'

It was strange to set foot in a fortress again. Esca and Marcus waited as a cohort of soldiers on horse-back rode by. Suddenly Vipsania, Marcus's horse, felt the pull of her old life. She turned quickly and tried to follow. Marcus had little power still in his right leg. It took a few moments before he could stop her and bring her back.

The soldiers laughed. 'Never bring a stolen Legion horse into a fortress,' said one. 'You must remember that.'

Marcus looked at him coldly. 'I, Demetrius of Alexandria, *the* Demetrius of Alexandria, do not steal horses, my good man. And if I did, I should steal a better one than this.'

'You can see the Legion's mark on her shoulder, clear as day,' said the other.

'But if you can't also see, as clear as day, that it's been written

43

over,' Marcus answered, 'you must need my "New Eyes Medicine". I can let you have a small pot for a price.'

Everyone laughed again.

'Are there not enough bad eyes for you here in the south?' the soldier asked. 'Why do you have to go up north to find more?'

'Maybe I am like Alexander,' said Marcus. 'I am looking for fresh worlds to win.'

'Well,' said the other. 'The old world is good enough for me – where you can live to enjoy it.'

'No sense of adventure, that's your trouble,' Marcus said. 'Now how do you think I became *the* Demetrius of Alexandria, of the New Eyes Medicine, the most famous eye-doctor between Caesarea and—'

'Quiet! Here comes the Commander,' somebody said; the soldiers went quickly about their business and Marcus and Esca were shown out.

The Wall was behind them and they rode out to the north. Chilurnium looks a nice place for a fortress, Marcus thought, looking round at the woods of the valley and the quiet river. There would be fishing, swimming and good hunting in times of peace.

He and Esca rode together in silence over the grass. There were no roads here. There seemed to be no living thing either. The hills looked wild and lonely.

Late that afternoon they stopped by a river to rest. The water ran clear over white stones. The horses drank, and so did Marcus and Esca.

They lay back under some trees in flower. It's good to be here, Marcus thought, after all those days of making plans, and waiting. Now they only needed to put the plan into action. They were going to work their way north from coast to coast. That way they should cover all the ground. Somewhere they must cross the way the Legion and the Eagle went.

Am I trying to do too much? Marcus thought to himself as he looked at the great spaces of wild country around him. But his heart lifted. I shall do it! he thought. I shall bring the lost Eagle back to Eburacum. My father's legion will live again, with a clean name before the world.

Esca broke the silence. 'So the hunting is to begin at last.'

'The hunting-ground is a wide one,' Marcus said. 'Who knows where it may lead us? Esca, you know this country better than I. So, if you tell me to do a thing, I shall do it, and will not ask you why.'

'That makes sense,' Esca said.

Marcus looked up at the sun. 'We must move on soon, I suppose. We have not yet found this village we are looking for.' It was not safe to go to a strange village after dark, even south of the wall.

'We shall not have far to look,' Esca said, 'if we follow the river down.'

'What tells you that?' Marcus asked.

'Smoke. Over that hill. I saw some a little while ago.'

'Come, then.' Marcus got up.

All that summer Marcus and Esca travelled through Valentia, crossing from coast to coast and pushing slowly to the north. They ran into no trouble. Everyone accepted Marcus as the eye-doctor he said he was. Many people needed his medicines. Marcus did a good job. He had gentle hands and was kind to the sick.

Usually somebody in each village gave them food and a bed for the night. If the way to the next village was dangerous or difficult to find, a hunter took them there.

One hot, late summer's day Marcus and Esca sat side by side and looked down at the sea. Marcus was worried. 'We have come too far north,' he said. 'We are nearly in Caledonia.'

'But the Eagle is more likely to be there,' said Esca. 'The Painted People would not leave it in a land which is Roman, if only in name.'

'I know,' Marcus said, 'but there should be some sign of it or the Legion by now. We have heard and seen nothing. And it will be much harder among the mountains of Caledonia.'

They were silent for a moment. Then Marcus took a coin from his bag. 'We will let the gods decide,' he said. 'If it's heads, we'll go on; if it's ships, we'll go south.' He threw the coin into the air. 'Ships it is,' he said. 'We turn south again.' So they did.

A few nights later they reached the old fort of Agricola, at the Place of the Three Hills. Thirty years ago this was a busy fort. But now nature was in command: grass covered the streets, and the walls of the houses stood open to the rain. Nobody lived here any more.

'If ever the Legions come north again, they will have a fine building job on their hands,' Marcus said, as the two men looked around. It was strangely silent.

'I do not like this place,' said Esca, half under his voice.

'We will make a fire,' said Marcus. 'That will keep any wild animals off.'

'It is not animals I am afraid of,' said Esca.

'What, then?'

Esca tried to laugh. 'I am a fool. Maybe the voices of the past. A lost Legion.'

Marcus looked at him sharply. 'It was a Cohort of the Twentieth Legion here. Never the Ninth.'

'How do we know where the Ninth went,' Esca said, 'after they marched out of sight?'

Marcus was silent for a moment. 'I don't think they will hurt us, even if they do come,' he said at last. 'And this is a good place to sleep. But if you say the word, we will go out to the woods.'

'No, we will stay here,' Esca said quickly.

They passed a good evening by the fire before lying down to sleep. But in the early hours of the morning Esca woke Marcus. 'Listen,' he said softly.

Marcus listened. He went cold. Somebody – or something – was singing. He knew the song well. It was an old marching song of the Legions.

'Oh, when I joined the Eagles,
(And it seems like yesterday)
I kissed a girl at Clusium
Before I marched away.'

Marcus went to the doorway. The voice came nearer. Suddenly the singer came round a corner. Marcus stopped in surprise. For the man was one of the Painted People.

The man stopped too and held his hunting-spear as if for

46

attack. For a moment they looked at each other in the early morning light.

Then Marcus spoke, in the language of the North People. 'You've had good hunting, friend,' he said, pointing to a dead animal across his horse's back.

'Good enough until I can do better,' said the man. 'There is none to give you.'

'We have food of our own,' Marcus said. 'Also we have a fire. You are welcome to join us.'

'What are you doing here in the Place of the Three Hills?' asked the man.

'We are just spending the night. It is free to all, is it not?'

For a moment the man did not speak. Then he put down his spear. 'Are you the eye-doctor I have heard of?' he said.

'I am.'

'I will come and join you.'

The stranger was a man of middle age, thin and powerful. He wore only a yellow-coloured skirt. In the light of the fire they saw the blue marks all over his body and arms. He was certainly one of the Painted People.

He began to cut the meat and put it in the fire.

Marcus watched him closely. He could not understand it. How does one of the Painted People come to be singing, 'The Girl I Kissed at Clusium'? he asked himself.

'Thank you for the heat of your fire,' the man said. He spoke less roughly now. 'My name is Guern, I am a hunter, as you see.'

'And I am Demetrius of Alexandria, a travelling eye-doctor, as you seem to know, and this, my friend, is Esca Mac Cunoval of the Brigantes,' Marcus said with a smile. He waited a moment then said, 'Where did you learn that song, friend – Guern the hunter?'

'Where else but here?' said Guern. 'When this was a Roman fort many Roman songs were sung here. I was only a boy but I remember well. And where did *you* learn it?'

'I have worked in many fortress towns before now,' Marcus answered. 'I have a quick ear for a song.'

Guern turned the meat in the fire. 'Yet you do not look old enough.'

'I began early,' Marcus said, 'following in my father's steps. Are there any bad eyes in your village?'

'I live outside the village,' Guern said, 'and my family has no bad eyes. But if you wait until my hunting is finished you are welcome to come with me. We will eat together and later I will show you the way to another village.'

For a moment Marcus wondered what to do. Then, certain that this man was not what he seemed, he accepted.

'We will come, and gladly.'

Then the three of them ate the fresh meat together, as friends. A day later they set out to the west.

I I

'This is my house,' said Guern the Hunter. They stopped in front of a large hut high up in the hills. 'You may stay as long as you please.'

A girl child sat playing before the door. A small boy watched over the cows and looked at the strangers with fear in his eyes.

Marcus bent double to pass through the small doorway. Inside blue smoke made his eyes water. A woman rose from the fire at the centre.

'Murna, I have brought home the eye-doctor and his friend,' said Guern.

'They are very welcome,' said the woman, 'but, thanks to the gods, there are no bad eyes here.'

Marcus sat down and watched the woman as she bent over a large metal pot on the fire. She was much younger than Guern: a tall woman with a happy face. Her clothes were of a rough material, but there were jewels on her dress and in her hair. These, and the metal pot, showed that Guern was not a poor man.

Esca and Guern now came in, followed by the children. The woman brought the men their meal, then returned to eat her own on the far side of the fire, the woman's side. They were a nice little family, yet it was strange that they lived outside the village. Something else unusual, Marcus thought. The song — and now this. . . .

The next morning, as Guern was washing, Marcus noticed a small mark on his face under the hair. It was the mark of Mithras; Marcus too had one, now hidden under his long hair. It was burned into the skin when the soldiers first joined the Eagles. So, thought Marcus, that's it. Now I'm quite sure. When the right moment comes I will ask him about it.

Later they set out for the next village. 'Is it two days' ride away,' Guern told them, 'so I will ride with you the first day and spend the night with you.'

That evening, many miles to the west, the three of them ate their meal under some rocks. Then they sat together round their small fire. Marcus looked across at the blue far-off hills towards Caledonia. Is the Eagle there? he wondered.

He turned to Guern. 'Soon, very soon now, our ways part,' he said, 'but before you go I want to ask you a question.'

'Ask then,' said the other.

Marcus said slowly, 'How did you become Guern the Hunter, when once you were with the Eagles?'

There was a long moment's silence. Guern looked hard at Marcus. 'Who told you that?' he asked at last.

'No one. I learnt by a song and the mark of Mithras on your face.'

There was another long silence. Then Guern said in a low voice,' I was once Sixth Centurion of the First Cohort of the Spanish Legion. Now go and tell it to the nearest Commander on the Wall. I shall not stop you.'

'I shall not tell,' said Marcus, 'for this reason.' He pushed his hair back and showed his own mark. 'Look!'

The other bent forward. 'So,' he said slowly. 'Who are you? Who are you?' He put his hands on Marcus and pulled him round. For a long moment he held him so. Esca got up quietly, his hand on his spear.

'I have seen you before,' said Guern in a rough voice. 'I remember your face. In the Name of Light, who are you?'

49

'Maybe it's my father's face you remember. He was your Cohort Commander.'

Guern's hands dropped to his side. His eyes never left Marcus's face. 'What are you doing here, in Valentia?' he asked. 'You are not from Alexandria, and I think you are not an Eye-Doctor.'

'No, I am not. But the medicines I carry are good, and I know how to use them.' Then, in a few words, Marcus explained why he was there. 'So when I realized you were different from the other hunters of the Painted People,' he finished, 'I hoped perhaps you could answer my questions.'

'What do you want to know?' Guern said after a moment.

'What became of my father's Legion? Where is the Eagle now?'

'I can answer the first of your questions, at least in part,' he said, 'but it is a long story. First I will put some more wood on the fire.'

Marcus's heart began to go faster and suddenly he felt a little sick.

'The seeds of death were in the Spanish Legion even before it marched north that last time,' Guern began, sitting back as the fire smoked up again. 'Boudicca, Queen of the Iceni, cut the Legion to pieces, sixty years ago, and called down the anger of her gods upon it. The Legion was formed again, but it never had the same heart in it. Things were always going wrong, men fell sick all the time; the Spanish never felt happy here. So it went from bad to worse. When I joined the Legion as a Centurion, two years before the end, it was already in a very bad condition.' Guern the Hunter shook his head.

'The last Legate was a hard man without understanding – he was the worst man to lead such a Legion. Then the British rose. The whole north was on fire. It was too much for a good Legion to manage, let alone a bad one. We fought back the Brigantes, and the Iceni, then we were ordered up to Valentia to keep out the Caledonians. Two of our cohorts were in Germany; with many of our men killed already, we left Eburacum for the North with well under four thousand.

'It was autumn, and the mountain country was covered in low

cloud. We could never see the Painted People coming, so they made attacks all the time. Well, by the time we reached the North Wall another thousand of us were dead. We chose a leader to speak to the Legate, and asked to return. "Let us leave Valentia to the Painted People," he said "for it is no more than a name. The men are down at heart – they cannot take any more." But the Legate said no.

'As a result, more than half of the men turned against the Legate and began to fight,' Guern turned from the fire to look at Marcus. 'I was not among them. But it ended badly. The Legate was killed – and then the British came over the walls and joined in the fighting.

'By next morning there were only two cohorts left alive in the fort. The rest were not all dead, oh no. Many of them went back over the walls with the Painted People. They may be in Caledonia now, for all I know, living as I do myself, with a British wife, and sons to come after them.

'Your father called those of us who were left together. We decided to fight our way out of the old fort and carry the Eagle back to Eburacum.

'That night those outside were eating and drinking heavily. We got out by the south and passed them by in the dark and the low cloud and began the march back.

'They followed us at first light and hunted us. It was like a sport to them. Have you ever been hunted? All day we pushed on, but many had to drop out, and die. Then I dropped out too.' Guern touched his leg. 'There was a hole in my leg this wide,' he held up three fingers, 'and I was sick. I took my chance at nightfall and hid in some trees. Then I walked all night. At first light I came to a village.

'The people in the first hut took me in and looked after me. Murna looked after me. They did not seem to care that I was a Roman soldier. A few nights later I saw the Eagle carried by on its way north again; now it was in the hands of the Painted People.'

'How far did the Romans get?' Marcus asked.

'I don't know. But they never reached Trinomontium. I looked there again and again and found no signs of fighting.'

'And my father?'

'He was with the Eagle when I dropped out. There were no Romans with it when they carried it north again.'

'Where is the Eagle now?' Marcus asked.

'I don't know,' Guern said, 'but tomorrow, when there is light to see by, I will give you what direction I can.'

Marcus did not sleep much that night. His dream was over, he realized now. What a fool he was! Just because it was my father's Legion, he thought. I was so sure there was never anything wrong with it. I know better now. It was bad – through and through. Oh my poor father! How terrible he must have felt.

But, I still have to find the Eagle and bring it back. It mustn't be left in the hands of the Painted People. I still have a job to do.

The next morning Guern and Marcus stood side by side and looked to the north-west. 'Cross the river over there where the valley opens,' Guern said, 'then two days' march, three at the most, will bring you to the old north line.'

'And then?'

'I can tell you only this: the men who carried the Eagle north were of the Epidaii people. They live among the mountains of the west coast.'

'Do you have any idea where their Holy Place may be?'

'No.'

They were silent for a moment. Esca brought up the horses. Then Guern said quickly, 'Do not go that way. It leads into the mouth of death.'

'I must take my chance of that,' Marcus said, 'And you, Esca?'

'I go where you go,' Esca answered.

'Why?' Guern asked. 'Now you know the truth. They will not form the Legion again. Why go on?'

'I must still bring back the Eagle,' Marcus said.

Guern looked down. 'Oh why did you come? I was happy with my woman – my new life. Now I feel bad because I let you go north alone.'

'There is no need for you to feel that,' Marcus said. 'Two men are better than three for work such as this. Go back to your people, Guern. And thank you for answering my questions.'

He jumped on to his horse. A few moments later he and Esca were riding towards the river.

12

One evening more than a month later Marcus and Esca stopped to rest their tired horses. They were at the top of a line of mountains looking over the sea to the west. It was a lovely evening. A gentle wind played on the water. To the north the dark mountain Cruachan rose into the clouds.

Marcus was used to this country now. They saw mountains and water – lakes or the sea – everywhere they went. But never a sign of the Eagle. Marcus was down at heart. There were so many holy places along the coast. Yet nowhere did anyone speak of the lost Eagle. He felt like giving up hope.

Suddenly he heard Esca's voice. 'Look, there are people on the road.'

He looked back. A party of hunters was climbing towards them. Marcus turned Vipsania, and waited for them to come up. There were five men in all. Two of them carried a dead animal. Dogs ran at their feet.

They were different from the men of Valentia. They were darker and smaller.

'You have had good hunting,' Marcus said.

'We have,' agreed their leader.

'Have you any people with eye-sickness in your village?' Marcus asked out of habit.

The man looked interested. 'Do you know how to make eyes better?'

'Do *I* know how to? I am Demetrius of Alexandria. *The* Demetrius of Alexandria,' said Marcus. 'I am an eye-doctor.'

'We do have some people with bad eyes,' said the man. 'Can you make them better?'

'How do I know until I see them?' Marcus said. 'Are you going to the village now? Let us go together.'

And on they went. At last they came down through some woods to a great lake, among the hills. It was nearly dark when they reached the village.

Marcus followed the leader into a large living-hut. Inside, it was very hot and full of blue smoke. A tall girl in a straight green dress appeared from behind a curtain of animal skins.

'Supper is ready and waiting,' she said.

'Let it wait a while longer, Fionhula, my heart,' said Dergdian. 'I have brought home an eye-doctor. So bring him the little boy.'

The woman's dark eyes moved quickly to Marcus's face. There was a kind of surprised hope in them. She turned without a word. A few moments later she was back, holding a little boy of about two in her arms.

Marcus saw that his eyes were big and red: the child could not open them.

'Here is one for you to make better,' said Dergdian.

'Yours?' Marcus asked.

'Mine.'

'He will lose his sight,' said an old man by the fire. 'I have always said so. I am never wrong.'

Marcus took no notice. 'Give the little boy to me,' he commanded. 'I will not hurt him.' He took the child. 'There, little boy, I won't take long. Let me look. What have you been putting in this child's eyes?'

'Animal fat,' said the old man. 'With my own hands, though it is woman's work, for my grandson's wife is a fool.'

'Has it done any good?'

'Maybe not,' said the old man.

'Then why use it?'

'Well, we always do in these parts. All women do. Except my grandson's wife.' His face showed what he thought of her.

The girl behind Marcus caught her breath. He felt angry too. But there was no point in making an enemy of the old man. So he said, 'We will see. Since the animal fat has not worked yet, I will try my own medicines.'

54

He turned to Fionhula. 'Bring me warm water, and a light,' he said, and set to work.

Marcus and Esca remained for many days in Dergdian's hut. The child's eyes were worse than usual, and Marcus wanted to stay till they were better — if only to prove the old man wrong.

The days went very slowly. He had much time on his hands. He listened hard to the stories the men told round the fire in the evenings. But he never heard anything of the Eagle.

From time to time he saw the black cloak of a Druid pass through the village. The Druids did not live among the people but out in the forests and mountains. No one spoke of them.

Then one evening he found Dergdian cleaning a heavy war-spear. Marcus watched, and remembered another war-spear.

Soon Dergdian looked up. 'It's for the Feast of the New Spears,' he said, 'for the dancing of the war-men that comes afterwards.'

'The Feast of the New Spears?' Marcus repeated. 'That's when your boys become men, isn't it? I have heard of such a feast, but never seen it.'

'You will see it in three nights from now, on the night of the New Moon,' Dergdian said. 'It's a great feast. The boys come from all over our land, and their fathers with them. Even the King's son must come to us, when it is time for him to receive his spears.'

'Why?' Marcus asked, with great interest.

'We are the keepers of the Holy Place,' said Dergdian, turning the spear. 'We watch over the Life of the People.'

'So,' said Marcus, 'and may anyone watch this mystery of the New Spears?'

'Not the mystery, no. That is between the New Spears and the Great One. Only the Holy Men may see it and live. But anyone may watch what they do before and after. Except the women.'

'Then, if I may, I shall choose to be there. We Greeks — we are born asking questions,' Marcus said.

By evening the next day the first New Spears were coming in: boys and their fathers from far parts of the land. They rode fine horses and were wearing their brightest clothes. There was soon a great crowd down by the lake-side.

On the second evening the boys disappeared. Marcus did not see them go, but suddenly they were gone. The men and the women who were left behind took their evening meal together sadly. Tears covered their cheeks. They seemed to think the boys were dead.

But the next morning they were all at peace again. There was a great sense of waiting in the village. Then, towards evening, the men went down to the lake in groups.

The women stood apart from the men. Many of the young ones wore late summer flowers in their hair. From time to time they all looked up into the sky at the south-west.

The sky was still golden, but the sun was now below the hills.

Then suddenly, there it was, the new moon, silver on the edge of the sunset. A girl saw it first and sang out a strange cry. The other women sang out too, and then the men.

At once the crowd broke up. The men moved off in the direction of the hills. The women stayed in the village.

Marcus followed the men, keeping close to Liathan, Dergdian's brother. He was suddenly very glad to know that Esca was walking behind him in this strange crowd.

They climbed up and over two mountains. Then they came to a wide valley, running up from the sea. At the head of the valley was a small round hill. There weas a great circle of standing stones around it. They stood out clearly in the gold of the sunset and the silver of the new moon.

'This is the Place of Life!' Liathan said in Marcus's ear. 'The Life of our People.'

The crowd turned to the north and made its way along the valley to the Place of Life. The round hill rose higher. Soon Marcus found himself among the Wolf People, in the shadow of one of the great standing stones. Before him was a wide empty space, covered with flat stones. Beyond that, in the side of the hill, was a doorway, made of age-old stone. A doorway from one world into another, Marcus thought. It was closed only by a curtain of skins. Was the lost Eagle of the Spanish Legion somewhere in there?

There was a sudden sound of fire. Young war-men were lighting torches. They carried them high above their heads and lit up the stones. A red-gold light fell on the doorway.

The curtain was thrown back. A man stepped out. He wore nothing except the skin of a grey wolf. It's head was pulled over his own.

The Wolf People shouted loudly. For a moment the man – Wolf Holy-Man, or Man-Wolf – stood before them. Then he moved to one side. Another man jumped out of the doorway – he was a bird. One after another they came, their bodies painted with strange colours and their backs covered with animal skins. In some strange way the men became, for the moment, the animals whose skins they wore.

There was one for each group of the Epidaii people. With excited shouts they formed into a circle and danced, quicker and quicker, round and round in a wheel. At last with a wild cry they fell back.

A man stood along in the doorway, caught in the full red light of the torches. A strangely tall and beautiful Holy-Man. He wore only a large head-dress of animal bones.

A great power seemed to come from him. Even Marcus felt it. The man held his hands high.

A deep shout rose from the people until they sounded like wolves crying to the moon. 'The Great One! The Great One!' They fell on their faces. Marcus did so too.

When they rose again, the Holy-Man god was speaking. 'Your sons have died as boys,' he said, 'but now they are born again – as men of war.' He turned and called.

A red-haired boy stepped out into the light. The people shouted their welcome. Another followed, and another. Soon fifty or more New Spears stood before the crowd.

I wonder what happened to them in the dark, Marcus thought, and remembered the time when he received his mark of Mithras.

After the last boy came one more Holy-Man. The crowd shouted even louder as the curtain fell into place behind him. But to Marcus everything suddenly seemed very still. For the last man was carrying the Eagle.

13

A man stepped out from the crowd, his body painted as for war. He carried a spear. At the same time a boy walked forward. Father and son met in the centre of the open space. The boy took the spear from his father's hand. Then he turned to show himself to the people, before following his father. He joined the other war-men for the first time.

Another boy stepped out, and another. But they were only shadows in the corner of Marcus's eye. For he was still looking at the Eagle. The crowns and golden leaves, won in war by the Legion, were gone from the standard. The Eagle's great silver wings were lost too. But to Marcus it was still the Eagle of his father's Legion.

He saw very little else, until at last the Eagle was carried back into the dark. Then the crowd, led by the New Spears, moved back to the village. As they came back down the mountain the smell of cooking meat rose from below. Great fires burned outside the village. The women joined hands and ran to meet their men.

Now was the time to feast. Everyone began to eat the meat with great hunger. The women brought round large pots of a strong yellow wine. Soon the crowds were loud and happy, laughing and shouting as they ate and drank.

Marcus wanted quiet. He wanted to think. What was he to do about the Eagle?

Then, quite suddenly, the feast was over. The noise stopped. Men and women moved back, and dogs and children came up. The torches were lit again.

Marcus turned to Dergdian's grandfather. 'What happens now?'

'Dancing now,' said the other. 'See . . .

Even as he spoke a group of young war-men ran into the

circle of torches and began to bend and jump in the strange movements of a war-dance.

Dance followed dance. Only the women did not dance at all. Then came the Dance of the New Spears. The young boys stood in a line opposite their fathers.

'We too dance like this,' Esca told Marcus, 'We the Brigantes, on the night our boys become men.'

On his other side the old man Tradui bent towards Marcus. 'Don't your people hold the Feast of the New Spears?'

'We hold a feast,' Marcus said, 'but it's not like this. All this is strange to me. I have seen many things tonight that make me wonder.'

'So? – and what things?' the old man was quite friendly to-night after the wine. 'I will explain them to you if you wish.'

So with careful questions Marcus began to ask and listen. It was slow work, but little by little he found out from the old man all he needed to know.

The Holy-Men, it seemed, lived in the woods below the Place of Life. None watched over the Holy Place.

'Why should they?' said the old man. 'The Place of Life is watched over by the gods. Who would dare steal anything from the Great One?'

He talked easily now, and told many stories of his past, as old men will. And then he told how the Eagle was won, ten or twelve autumns ago.

'I was there,' said the old man with shining eyes. 'Some say I was too old even then. But I was not. It was my last fight. But what a fight! We closed round the last few Romans like wolves. We did not think it would be difficult. The others gave up so easily. But these last ones were stronger. They fought to the very last man. They held the god with the wings up high among them, and killed many of our men. We pulled them down at last until there were only ten left. I, Tradui, killed with my spear the holy man with the Eagle. But another caught it from him as he fell. This man was a leader among the rest. He wore the red cloak of war. He held the Eagle-god high and spoke brave words to the rest. I wished to be the one to kill him. But someone else was before me. . . .

59

'Well, we made an end. We left them to the wolves. And we brought back the Eagle-god. We the Epidaii. But there was heavy rain later. The river came down very full and as we crossed it the god was carried away by the water. We found it again later but the wings were lost from it, and the crowns and the leaves.

'We brought it to the Place of Life and offered it up to the Great One. He was clearly well pleased, for all our wars have gone well ever since, and we have had good hunting.'

The bright old eyes turned at last to Marcus's face. 'He was like you, that Roman leader with the Red Cloak. And yet you say you are a Greek. That is very strange.'

'There are many of Greek blood among the Roman soldiers,' Marcus answered.

'So. That might be it,' the old man began to look for something under his cloak. 'They were good war-men, I will say that. I took this from that leader – and I have carried it ever since.'

It was a ring. The green stone shone in the firelight. Marcus looked closely at it, taking it into his hand. He held it gently for a long moment. And in that moment it seemed he was looking up at his father once more. The dark, laughing face bent over him. The ring on his hand shone green in the sunlight as he pushed back his hair.

Marcus gave the ring back to the old man with a quick word of thanks, and looked back at the dancers.

But he was no longer interested in them. All at once he was tired – tired to the bottom of his heart.

The next day Marcus made his plans with Esca. And then he went to see Dergdian. 'We must go south again, tomorrow,' he said, 'before the winter closes in.'

Dergdian did not want him to go, but Marcus stood his ground. Now was the time, he said, now, after the Feast of the New Spears, when everyone else was leaving too.

Marcus and Esca spent the last day quietly. That evening they bathed in the cold waters of the lake. Then at sunset Marcus called on Mithras to watch over them. They ate little at the evening meal.

When the time came for sleep they lay down as usual with Tradui and the dogs and Liathan in the great living-hut. They were nearest the door.

Marcus did not sleep. At midnight Esca touched him lightly. They got up silently and left the hut, and the village.

It was a very still night. There was no moon. As they went down into the valley of the Place of Life everything was black around them like water.

They reached the round hill and stood for a long time to listen for any sound. But the silence was complete. They passed between the standing stones and stood before the doorway.

Marcus said softly but very clearly 'In the Name of Light' and lifted the skin curtain back. They entered. The black darkness seemed to press against their eyes. The place seemed alive, like a waiting animal.

Then Esca brought out a torch from under his cloak and made a light. He gave it to Marcus. He held the fire high and they walked forward. There were walls of stone close on either side of them.

Then at last they came into a great round room. A gold cup filled with dark red blood was set on a stone at the entrance. Opposite, against the far wall, something shone golden. It must be the Eagle, Marcus thought.

The rest of the place was empty.

They made their way round the room and reached the far wall. Yes, it was the Eagle.

'Take the torch,' Marcus said under his breath.

He lifted the Eagle from its place. The last Roman hand to touch this standard was my father's, he thought. He began to pull the Eagle off the standard.

'Hold the light this way – a little higher. Yes, keep it so.'

Esca did so. But the job was not easy. Marcus began to feel afraid. Would he have time to do it? His breath came quickly. His hands were hot and wet.

The fire burned low and the light grew less. He looked at Esca. Esca returned his look. Neither of them spoke. Their fear was too great.

At last he managed it. The Eagle came off. Now he would be

61

able to carry it back easily under his cloak. Marcus put the standard back against the wall. Then they moved quickly round the room and made for the entrance. Esca covered their footmarks.

It seemed to take for ever. But suddenly Esca's shadow fell on to the curtain. They were there.

'Get ready to put out the light,' Marcus said. Esca did so and Marcus carefully pulled the curtain back. There was no sign of danger. Quickly they came out into the clean night air. Esca was shaking. Marcus put his hand on his friend's arm.

'We are out,' he said,' we are through. It is over. It's all right, old wolf.'

Esca answered him with a shaky laugh. 'I want to be sick.'

'So do I,' Marcus said, 'but we have no time just now. The Holy Men may find us. Come.'

Some time later they came out of the woods on the edge of the lake. Esca took off his clothes. 'Now give me the Eagle.' He took it, and a moment later Marcus was alone.

He heard a sound like a fish, jumping in the water. Then all was silent again. He waited for what seemed a very long time.

Then suddenly Esca was beside him again, his hair and body wet.

'Well?' asked Marcus.

'I have found a good place for it,' Esca told him, 'under a stone at the water's edge. They may search till the lake runs dry, and never find it. But I shall know the place when I come again.'

They returned to the village. All was quiet. But they were not a moment too soon. The smell of early morning was on the air.

As they made their way silently through the doorway of the hut, the dying fire shone like red jewels in the darkness. One of the dogs made a low noise, half asleep.

Liathan moved. 'What is it?' he asked in his sleep.

'It is only I,' Marcus said. 'I thought I heard Vipsania moving. I went out to see to her.'

He lay down. Esca also lay down, near the fire to dry his hair. Silence came again to the sleeping hut.

14

A few hours later Marcus and Esca left the village. They went south at first, following the edge of the lake to its foot. Then they turned north-east through the mountains. By evening they came to another lake – a long sea-lake this time.

That night they slept in a small village, and the next day they set out for another village at the head of the lake.

They rode easily all that day, and rested the horses often. Marcus wanted to get as far away as possible from this land of sea-lakes and mountains. But there was no point in hurrying. They must wait for their followers to catch up with them.

For the Holy Men would know the Eagle was gone by now. The village people would think of Marcus and Esca as the most probable thieves. They would be up and after them by now.

But they took longer to come than Marcus thought. At last his ear caught the sound of horses. Looking back he saw six or seven horsemen racing down a mountainside towards them.

'Here they come at last,' he said to Esca, 'listen to the dogs.'

Esca laughed quietly. 'Do we ride on or wait for them?'

'Wait for them,' Marcus decided. 'They will know we have seen them.'

A few minutes later the horsemen arrived. Dergdian and his brother were among them. Marcus took in their ugly looks and the war-spears they carried. He looked hurt. 'Dergdian? Liathan? What do you want with me, and in such a hurry?'

'You know very well what we want,' Dergdian said. His face was set like a stone.

'But I'm afraid I don't,' said Marcus. 'You will have to tell me.'

'Yes, we will tell you,' an older hunter cut in. 'We come to take back the Eagle-god, and also for your blood.'

The others pressed in on the two men, shouting wildly.

63

Marcus looked surprised. 'The Eagle god?' he repeated. 'The one we saw at the Feast of the New Spears? Why – have you lost it?'

'It has been stolen,' Dergdian said very softly.

'And you think I stole it?' Marcus's eyes opened wide. 'Why should I want a Roman Eagle?'

'You may have your reasons,' said Dergdian.

'I can't think of any.'

There were shouts of 'Kill! Kill!' from the men. They shook their spears before Marcus's eyes. 'Kill the thieves. There has been enough talking.'

'If you are so sure we are the thieves,' Marcus said quietly,' then search our bags. You will surely find it.'

They did so, quickly and roughly. Marcus and Esca watched as they threw their few things on to the ground. Cloaks, a cook-ing-pot, some smoked meat. One of the hunters pulled out the medicine-box.

Marcus said to their leader Dergdian, 'Will you ask them to be less rough with my medicines? There may be other bad eyes in the land, even if your son's eyes are better.'

Dergdian's face went red. Then he spoke sharply to the man. 'Take care with the medicines, you fool.'

Soon everything was out and on the ground.

'Well, are you still so sure?' asked Marcus. 'Or would you like to search us to the skin?'

Their eyes ran over him, over Esca. Clearly there was nothing of the size of the Eagle under their clothes.

Dergdian shook his head. 'We must look somewhere else, it seems.'

The seven men looked sorry now. Quietly they put the things back. They've pulled my ring-jewel almost out of my cloak, Marcus noticed. It has cut right through the material at the corner.

'Come back with us,' said Dergdian. 'We have not been good to you. Come back and we will be friends again.'

Marcus shook his head. 'We must go south before the year closes in. Good hunting to you this winter.'

He watched them go with a sad look in his eyes.

'Do you wish the Eagle was still in the Place of Life?' Esca asked.

'No,' said Marcus, 'then it would still be a danger to the other Legions. But I feel badly about Dergdian and his men.'

They rode on. Soon they caught sight of the village at the head of the lake. It was not their first visit. A crowd of men and women, children and boys came up and called to them as they entered.

'It is time that I grew sick,' said Esca softly to Marcus. He half-closed his eyes, and fell on to his horse's neck. 'My head!' he said. 'My head is on fire.'

Marcus explained that Esca was sick. 'He must rest a few days,' he said, 'two or three days at the most. It is an old sickness. It returns from time to time.'

'You are welcome,' said the headman, 'please share my fireside.'

But Marcus shook his head. 'Give us some place to ourselves. It doesn't matter how rough it is, so long as it keeps out the weather. But it must be far from your living-huts. Your people must not see or touch him while he is ill, or they may fall sick too.'

The people talked the matter over quickly and then decided to give them a cow-hut outside the village. The men took their horses and the women brought food.

At last they were alone. Marcus and Esca looked at each other. 'We have done well, up to now,' said Marcus. Esca ate the last of his meat. Then he stood up, ready to go. He had Marcus's cloak under his arm.

At the last moment Marcus said, 'Oh, this leg of mine! I ought to go back, not you.'

Esca shook his head. 'It is safer for me, anyway. I am a born hunter.'

Marcus looked out at the dark mountains. 'All is clear,' he said. 'You are sure you can find the way?'

'Yes.'

'Good hunting, then, Esca.'

A dark shadow disappeared into the night. And Marcus was alone.

For three nights and two days Marcus kept watch over an empty hut. In the mornings and evenings a woman brought food and set it on a flat stone a little way off. Marcus slept when he could, but spent most of his time just inside the doorway watching the grey waters of the lake and the high mountains.

Autumn was in the wind. He could smell it. The leaves were turning gold and falling into the river.

On the third night a hand brushed across the skin curtain at the entrance. It was Esca.

'Is everything all right?' he asked softly.

'Fine,' Marcus answered, and made a light. 'And with you? How was the hunting?'

'The hunting was good,' Esca said. He set down something inside the cloak.

Marcus looked at it. 'Was there any trouble?'

'None.' He sat down, tired. 'Is there anything to eat?'

Marcus gave him some meat. Esca began to tell his story, in between hungry mouthfuls.

'I saw many war-men,' he said. 'I had to hide many times. They carried war-spears. But at last I managed to swim across the lake in the dark. I found the place quite easily and brought the Eagle back in the cloak. I came back as fast as I could. It was all very easy – almost too easy.'

Esca was falling asleep as he spoke. He finished eating and lay down at once. Sleep took him like a tired dog after a day's hunting.

But before the sun was above the mountains next day they were on their way once more. The village people did not seem surprised that Esca was suddenly better. They gave the travellers more smoked meat and a boy came with them to show them the way.

It was through difficult mountain country now. The boy left them at night-fall, and they sat down to rest, thankful that the worst was over.

It's a straight journey south now, Marcus thought. Only two days' march to Valentia. Yet he felt a little worried. It was all too easy, he thought. Perhaps there will be trouble yet.

He looked at the sky. There was a wonderful sunset. The whole sky to the west seemed to be on fire and the racing clouds changed from gold to red and from red to purple. A storm is on its way, he thought, wind and rain, and maybe something more. The red light on that mountain looks like blood. . . .

Oh, I'm a fool! Marcus shook himself in anger. I'm just tired, that's all. And I haven't even looked at the Eagle yet. I didn't like to in the village; but now . . .

It lay beside him. He pulled the edge of the cloak. There it was – the Eagle of the Ninth!

He took it in his hands. It was cold and heavy, and burned red-gold in the sunset.

'Now that's what I call good hunting, brother!' he said, looking up at Esca.

But Esca's eyes suddenly grew wide. He was looking at one corner of the cloak.

'Your ring-jewel!' Esca said. 'The ring-jewel!'

It was gone. Oh, what a fool I was, Marcus thought. I saw it was cutting through the cloak when those men pulled our things out so roughly. I forgot all about it afterwards. So did Esca, it seems.

'It may have fallen out at any time – even while you were in the water,' he said.

'No,' Esca said slowly. 'It rang on the stones when I put the cloak down – before I swam for the Eagle.' He thought hard. 'When I picked up the cloak it caught on the root of a tree at the water's edge. I remember now. At the time I didn't really notice.'

They sat quite still and looked at each other. It was an unusual ring-jewel. Every man in the village knew it belonged to Demetrius of Alexandria.

'If they find it they will know one of us has been back,' Marcus said. 'They will know there can only be one reason for that.' He began to put the Eagle back into the cloak.

'Listen, Marcus,' Esca said. 'You must push on alone. If you take Vipsania and go now, you may stand a chance. I will put myself in their way—'

'They will kill you,' Marcus said. 'No, we are in this together and we will win clear together, or not at all.'

He got to his feet. 'It may be days before they find the ring-jewel; but let's go down to Valentia now as fast as we can.'

Esca got up too. Marcus looked up at the wild clouds. 'How long before the storm breaks?' he asked.

The other seemed to be smelling the weather. 'Long enough to get down to the lake-side, anyway. We may manage a few more miles tonight.'

15

Two mornings later, Marcus lay on a low hill-top and looked down at the silver line of the river Cluta and the town of Are-Cluta. The blue hills of Valentia rose to the south. The sky was grey now, gentle after the wild storm.

I'm glad that's over, thought Marcus. What a journey! All that rain and wind and darkness. I don't know how we managed to get this far. But what is Esca doing? He should be back by now. It doesn't take this long to sell two horses. Marcus began to feel worried. Have they heard about the Eagle already in Are-Cluta?

It was nearly midday when Esca appeared. He was riding a rough little horse with long hair, and leading another.

'Do you call these wild animals horses?' Marcus asked with a smile.

'It was the best I could do,' answered Esca. 'And I got this as well. He shook out a dirty blue and red cloak. That and the horses should change the way we look, don't you think? Oh, and I got some dried meat. Here it is.'

They began to eat with great hunger. Marcus was sad at losing Vipsania and Minna. But they were too easy to recognize, with the Legion marks on their bodies. They had to go.

The two men finished their meal quickly. There was no time

to lose. Soon they were on their way again. This time Marcus was wearing the blue and red cloak. Under it he held the Eagle close to his body.

They travelled fast. The little horses were strong if not big. They were used to the mountains and quick on their feet. Marcus and Esca rested during the day, hiding among the trees, and rode through the night. For three days they saw and heard nothing. But they knew in their hearts that the hunt was on.

On the fourth evening they set out again, under a low grey sky.

'Three more days,' Marcus said suddenly. 'Three more days and we should reach the Wall!'

Esca looked round to answer and then suddenly his head went up. He was listening to something. Then Marcus heard it too, very far behind. It was a dog.

They were on the top of a low line of hills. Looking back, they saw some dark shapes on the line of hills behind them.

'I spoke too soon,' Marcus said. 'Men on horseback, and dogs. Lots of dogs.' At that moment another dog took up the cry.

'They have seen us,' Esca said. 'The hunt is on. Ride, brother!' And even as he spoke, his little horse jumped forward.

Marcus kicked his own, and together they raced forward.

'If we can keep going until dark,' Esca shouted, 'we've a chance among the trees of the higher ground ahead.'

Marcus did not answer, he just rode as never before. For one moment it seemed terribly exciting. Then that moment passed and he was riding for his life, with the hunt in full cry behind him. On and on they raced, over rough and difficult ground. Now the horses were getting tired.

The land was rising under them, and the light going fast. The woods were very near; but so was the hunt.

They came over the top of another hill and saw a small river below them. At the same time a sweet heavy smell rose up to them.

Esca cried out,' Down to the water before they come over the hill and we've a chance yet!'

Marcus did not quite understand, but he followed Esca. Side by side they raced down through the tall grass, the animal smell getting stronger every second.

Suddenly two large fighting animals broke out from some trees beside them and ran off down the valley.

Esca was already half off his horse, and he pulled Marcus off his. 'Into the water, quick!' Esca cried, while the two horses raced on into the dark without their riders.

The two men jumped into the ice-cold water just as the hunt came over the hill. Hiding under a rock, they heard the men, horses and dogs pass by like thunder. They were following the smell of Marcus's and Esca's horses.

The two men in the water watched the hunt disappear into the dark until every sound was gone. Now all they heard was the call of a bird and the racing of their own hearts.

Esca rose quickly to his feet. 'Our horses will go like the wind for a while,' he said, 'free of us as they are. But the hunt will run them down and then it will come back to look for us. So we must get away fast.'

Marcus made sure the Eagle was still safe. 'I feel sick about those horses,' he said.

'The dogs will not kill them unless the word is given. And Britons do not waste horses,' said Esca. 'We must keep to the water for a while,' he said.

They fought their way against the water for a very long time, or so it seemed to Marcus. It was quite dark now, and the hills closed round them. At last they climbed out, with ice-cold legs and feet, shook themselves like dogs, and set off again.

After some time they sat down to rest in a small wood. They kept close together to get warm. Their food was with the horses, so from now on they would have to march empty. They were still at least two full days' march from the nearest station on the Wall.

Marcus's leg was hurting badly. He felt as if the whole land was awake and hunting, the dark hills themselves closing in for the kill.

They sat silent a short while longer, to get their breath back. But they did not dare to rest long. Marcus was just getting to his feet, when Esca touched him. Someone or something was moving, far down the valley.

Marcus stayed where he was, his head turned to listen. The sounds came nearer. It might be one man or a few. It was difficult to tell.

The sound came slowly up the valley towards them. Marcus looked through the leaves, and made out a white shape and a dark one. It was a man leading a cow.

The man was singing softly to himself. They only heard the song when he was a few feet from them. It was one they knew well:

'O when I joined the Eagles,
(And it seems like yesterday)
I kissed a girl at Clusium
Before I marched away.'

Marcus reached up and lifted the leaves. 'Well met, Guern the Hunter,' he said in his own language.

16

The man looked up in surprise. 'Well met, Demetrius of Alexandria.'

'Guern, we need your help,' Marcus said quickly.

'Yes, I know. You have brought away the Eagle and the Epidaii are after you,' Guern said. 'The word went by at sunset. The Dumnonii and my own people at least will join spears with them.' He came a step nearer. 'What would you like me to do?'

'We want food – and a way back to the Wall.'

'I can manage the food, but the other is not so easy. They are watching every way south now. But I know of one they will leave open.'

'Tell us how to find it.'

'It is not enough to tell you. It would be death for you on your own.'

'And you know this way?' Esca spoke for the first time.

'Yes, I know the way. I – will take you by it.'

'But what if you are caught with us?' Marcus said, 'And won't you be missed from your own place?'

'I shall not be missed. Everyone is out hunting. And if anyone finds us together, I can always kill one of you. Then I can say I was the First Spear to find you.'

'A nice thought,' Marcus smiled. 'Do we come with you now?'

'Yes,' Guern decided. 'We will have to take the cow with us, I'm afraid.'

They set off, and climbed over many hills and through long valleys. It was nearly first light when Guern at last found them a place to rest for the day.

Marcus and Esca managed to sleep a little when they forgot their hunger. At last the light turned to gold. When it was dark Guern returned, bringing both fresh and smoked meat.

'Eat the fresh meat now,' he said, 'and quickly.'

They did as he said. Before it was completely dark they were on their way again.

They marched slowly at first, for Marcus's leg was still hurting. But the way was easier than the night before. They were going downhill now. They followed Guern, silent as shadows.

Then suddenly the air seemed to change; and with it, the feel of the ground under their feet. It was soft and wet. Marcus understood now. Guern was going to take them through water-fields. He must know of a hidden way.

They stopped at the edge of the grass and water. Guern was looking round him like a dog. 'Here. It's here,' he said, and spoke under his breath for the first time. 'From now on we must go behind one another. Follow me exactly, and never stop, even for a second. Even on the secret way the ground is soft. Do as I tell you and you will cross safely. If you do not, you will die.'

'We understand,' Marcus answered quietly.

Slowly they moved forward. There was a cold, wet smell. The moon went behind a cloud and they could see nothing. But Guern the Hunter walked on. On and on, over the soft ground. All was very silent.

How much longer? Marcus wondered Then, at last, he felt harder ground under his feet. Soon the secret way was behind them, like a bad dream.

Daybreak was near. They stopped under some trees and turned to look at each other.

'I have brought you as far as I can,' Guern said. 'Every man must keep to his own hunting-grounds. From now on the land is strange to me.'

'We will be able to manage now,' Marcus said quickly. 'Our enemies are behind us.'

Guern shook his head. 'Don't be too sure. They may search these hills also. So travel by night and rest by day. If all goes well you should reach the Wall in the second night from now.'

He looked at his feet, tried to speak, then was silent. At last he said, 'Before I leave you, I should like to see the Eagle once again. It was my Eagle once.'

Marcus took it out. 'It has lost its wings,' he said.

Guern reached out to take it, then let his hands fall back to his sides. 'So, I have seen the Eagle once more,' Guern said. 'Maybe I'll never see a Roman face again after today. . . . It's time you went.'

'Come with us,' Marcus said suddenly.

Guern lifted his head. Their eyes met. Then he shook his head. 'I am of the Selgovae now. I have a good wife. I have sons. My life is here. There is no way back.'

'Then – good hunting to you,' Marcus said, after a silence. 'Wish us well, between here and the Wall.'

'I do wish you well. If you win through, I shall hear of it and be glad.'

'We shall not forget your help,' Marcus said. 'The Light of the Sun be with you, Centurion.'

As they turned away, Esca said, 'He will hear if we come out of this alive, but we shall never hear if he does.'

'I wish he was with us,' Marcus said.

Two nights later, Marcus and Esca were still a long way from the Wall. The weather was bad and low cloud lay over the hills. It was difficult to see their way. Marcus's leg was giving him

73

trouble more often now. He said nothing and kept walking, but it was not easy for him.

At first light the clouds lifted for a moment. And they saw a man on horseback, high on a hill very near. He was clearly watching out for them. They fell flat on the grass. He did not see them, and Marcus and Esca saw him ride slowly away. Then the clouds came down again and hid him from sight.

They spent part of the day resting under a great rock, but set out again while there were still some hours of daylight left.

'How far have we still to go?' Marcus asked, as he tried out his bad leg.

'It's hard to say,' Esca answered. 'I should think twelve or fourteen of your Roman miles.'

Towards evening they felt a sudden wind. The low clouds began to break up. As the hills came into sight, a loud cry went up. A man on the other side of the valley ran out and climbed fast to the top of the hill.

Esca threw his spear after him. But it was too far. The man was already out of sight, calling to others.

'Down the hill!' Esca said in a rough voice. 'Into the woods!'

But even as they ran, they heard another cry rise up from the trees. There was no escape that way. There was only one way open to them. And that was straight up the hill to their right. They took it.

They reached the top and heard the call of the huntsmen behind them. Seeing a group of thick short trees just below, Marcus and Esca raced towards them. They had to lie flat to get in among the leaves and branches. Once under cover they lay among sharp roots and branches and listened. Their hearts were in their mouths.

The hunters came all round the trees. They pushed spears in among the branches, shouting all the time. This is it, thought Marcus, this must be the end.

Then, quite suddenly, the hunt left.

'They missed us!' Esca cried. Slowly the two men worked their way out into the open again.

They looked around. They were on the edge of a hill. There was no way down here. The rocky land fell sharply to a lake far below. Marcus turned to the north-west. But there were men waiting there. There seemed to be no way out. They could still hear the sounds of the hunt behind them.

'Over there!' said Marcus suddenly. 'Do you see that old building? I'm sure it's an old Roman look-out. Let's hide there.' They ran across to it.

Marcus and Esca went through the empty doorway. Dead leaves covered the floor. 'Up here!' cried Marcus, out of breath. He pointed to some stone stairs.

They climbed up, and the sound of their feet seemed very loud in the silence of the stone building. They came out through a low door on to the flat roof. As they did so, great black wings brushed Marcus's face. A bird flew up into the sky, with a loud cry. Now everyone will know we're here, Marcus thought.

But he was suddenly too tired to care very much. He looked out over the far side of the roof. Far below he could see the dark deep waters of the lake. Well, I can always throw the Eagle down there, he thought. At least that way it will never be used against the other Legions.

Esca was looking through a hole in the wall. 'They are still searching for us,' he said as Marcus came over to him. 'It's a good thing for us that they have no dogs. If they don't come up here before nightfall we may still escape them.'

'But they will come,' said Marcus. 'That bird has made sure of that. Listen. . . .'

Sounds came from the north of the hill. Someone was shouting in an excited way.

Marcus looked at Esca. 'I have won the Eagle. But I feel bad about you, Esca. What have you got from all this?'

Esca gave him a slow smile. There was a small line of blood on his neck. 'I have been a free man once again. I have had good hunting with my brother.'

Marcus smiled back at him. 'Yes, we have had good hunting.' The sounds were louder now. 'But I think that is all over now.' The horses came nearer.

Marcus felt very quiet. He thought of the Legate Claudius. Of Uncle Aquila in Calleva, of Cottia in the garden under the wild fruit trees. I wonder, will they ever know what happened to us, he thought. I'd like them to know how it was, at the end.

He felt almost happy. His eyes fell on a small wild flower, growing in a corner of the wall. It was very blue. The bluest thing I've ever seen, he thought.

Just then three shouting horsemen came over the hill and stopped outside the old walls.

17

'Only three up to now,' said Marcus in a low voice, as he and Esca hid below the walls. 'Don't use your knife unless you have to. They may be of more use to us living than dead.'

The three men soon came running up the stairs. But Marcus and Esca were both good fighters. They threw the first two men to the ground as they came out of the doorway. The third was more of a fighter, but Esca soon had him down and hit his head hard on the stone floor.

'Young fools,' he said, picking up a fallen spear. 'A young dog would know better than that.'

Two of the men – they were all very young – lay quite still; but one was already moving. Marcus bent over him. 'It is Liathan,' he said. 'I'll see to him. You tie up the other two.'

The young man opened his eyes. Marcus was holding a knife to his neck. 'That was a mistake,' Marcus said. 'Why didn't you keep with the rest of the hunt?'

Liathan looked up at him. His black eyes were hard with hate. Blood ran from the corner of his mouth. 'We saw the bird fly up. We wanted to be First Spear,' he said.

'I see. It was brave of you but very stupid.'

'Maybe. But there will be others here soon.'

'So,' Marcus said. 'When these others come you will tell them we aren't here. You will send them back the way they came.'

Liathan smiled. 'Why should I?' He looked at Marcus's knife. 'Because of that?'

'No,' said Marcus. 'Because when your friends come up the stairs, I shall throw the Eagle – here it is – down into the lake. We are still a long way from the Wall, and you will have other chances – you or others of the hunt – before we reach it. But if we die here, you will lose all chance of taking the Eagle-god back.'

For a long moment Liathan lay looking up at Marcus's face. In that silent moment they heard shouts and the sound of horses. Esca rose quickly and looked over the wall. 'The hunt is up,' he said softly. 'They are closing in, like wolves.'

'Choose,' Marcus said, very quietly to Liathan. He got up and moved to the wall, and took out the Eagle. The evening light shone on the wild, golden head.

Liathan walked over to the wall, and bent over it. The huntsmen were just arriving. He shouted down to them, 'They are not here, after all. Try the woods over there.'

Voices answered him, then the hunt turned back on itself.

Liathan turned once more to Marcus. 'I did that all right, didn't I?'

Marcus agreed. Suddenly Liathan jumped for his neck, like a wild cat. Marcus half-fell, with the Eagle under him. As he did so, Esca was upon Liathan, and brought him crashing down.

'You fool,' Marcus said a moment later, getting to his feet and looking down at Liathan. 'You young fool. There are two of us and only one of you.'

Esca tied Liathan up. Marcus looked across at the hills. The clouds were lifting now. The Wall was somewhere to the south of those hills, it could not be far now.

'Why did you come among us, calling yourself an eye-doctor. Why did you steal the Eagle-god?' Liathan's angry voice asked him.

Marcus turned. 'Well, am I not a good eye-doctor? But I came to take back the god – not *steal*, for it was never yours – because it was the Eagle of my father's Legion.'

'So my grandfather was right,' Liathan said.

'Was he? Tell me in what way?'

'When the Holy Men discovered the Eagle-god was gone, my

77

grandfather knew you were the thief. "He has the face of that Roman leader," he said, "I am sure he was his son!" But when we searched you and found nothing, we said grandfather was an old fool. Then Gault found your ring-jewel by the lake and a hole near the water-line. Later we heard a strange story from the village where your friend was sick. And my grandfather said, "I was right, after all. I'm never wrong." He sent for me and said, "If you find him, kill him if you can. But also give him his father's ring, for he is his father's son in more than blood." '

'You have it now?' Marcus said.

'You must take it for yourself since my hands are tied,' said Liathan. 'It's round my neck.'

Marcus found the ring. The great stone seemed a darker green now in the last light of the evening. 'When you go back to your own place, tell Tradui I thank him for my father's ring. We shall take two of your horses, now, Liathan, to carry us to the Wall, but we will turn them free when we have finished with them. I hope you find them later. Cover and tie his mouth now, Esca.'

Esca did so.

'I'm sorry,' Marcus said, as he met Liathan's angry eyes. 'But we can't let you shout for help yet. I am sure the other men will come back and find you soon.'

Esca picked up their spears and threw all but one over the wall into the lake. He kept one for himself. Then he and Marcus made for the stairs.

'The last stage,' said Marcus, as they climbed on to the horses. 'We will be at the Wall tomorrow morning.' He hoped he was right. For his leg was now hurting very badly.

They rode over the hill to the woods below.

'Thanks to the gods, the horses are still fresh,' said Esca. 'For we've a hard ride before us.'

'Yes,' said Marcus. The light was going fast now.

A long while later a soldier on the north wall of Borovicus thought he heard the sound of horses far below. He looked down but saw nothing. A cloud covered the moon and the wind was strong. It was only the wind, he thought, and continued to march up and down.

Some time later a voice cried, 'Open in the name of Caesar!' at the North Gate.

The soldier there was surprised. Not many people came from the north. And they certainly did not call out like that. He did not open up, but went up to the look-out above the gate. He saw two men below.

'Who asks to enter in Caesar's name?'

'We have important business with the Commander,' said one of the men. 'Open up, friend.'

The gates were slowly opened. In the yellow light the soldier looked over the two wild-looking men. One was half-carrying the other.

'Run into trouble, have you?' asked the soldier.

But the other laughed suddenly. Long rough hair covered his neck and face. He was black with dirt and blood, and thin as a stick.

'I wish to see the Commander at once,' he said, in the cool voice of a cohort centurion.

'What?' said the soldier in surprise. But he took Marcus to the Commander as he asked.

They reached a small, white room. 'Good evening, Drusillus,' Marcus said. 'I am glad you have done so well. A Commander yourself now, I see!'

The centurion did not understand.

'Do you not know me, Drusillus?' Marcus said. 'I am—'

But a light came into his old centurion's eyes. 'Centurion Aquila!' he said. 'Yes, sir, I know you. Of course I do! I would know you anywhere.'

He came round the table with a big smile. 'But what in the name of Thunder brings you here?'

Marcus put his cloak carefully on the table. 'We have brought back the Spanish Legion's lost Eagle,' he said, in a strange voice. Then very quietly, he fell forward on top of it.

18

Towards evening on a day in late October, Marcus and Esca rode up to Calleva. They were clean once more, and Marcus now had his hair short again, in the Roman fashion. But they still wore their old clothes, and were very thin and tired.

They rode into Calleva by the North Gate, left their horses and set out on foot for the house of Aquila. The yellow light in the windows seemed like a welcome. They pushed open the door. Old Stephanos was crossing the long hall and jumped in fear.

'It's all right, Stephanos,' Marcus told him, as he took off his wet cloak. 'It's only us. Is my uncle in his study?'

The old slave opened his mouth to answer, but they heard nothing. A wild, wolf-like sound filled the air. Suddenly a great grey shape threw itself through the doorway and raced across the floor to Marcus.

'Cub!' Marcus cried. He threw his arms round the young wolf's neck and Cub pushed his nose into his clothes. By this time the whole house knew of their return.

Marcipor and Sasticca came running, and Marcus smiled at them. 'You see we have returned after all, Marcipor! Sasticca, I have dreamed of your cooking night after night!'

'Ah, I thought I heard your voice, Marcus.'

There was a sudden silence. Uncle Aquila stood at the foot of the stairs, with his old grey dog at his side. Behind him was Claudius Hieronimianus, the Legate.

Marcus got up slowly. 'We have clearly arrived at a good time,' he began, as they shook hands hard. 'Uncle Aquila! Oh, it's good to see you again. How are things with you, sir?'

'Well enough – and even better now you are safely home again. But you look like something the cat's brought in,' said Uncle Aquila. 'Now – what news?'

'I have brought it back,' Marcus said quietly.

'He has done it!' Uncle Aquila said, with a big smile. 'He has done it, by all the gods! You didn't think he would, did you, Claudius?'

'I am not sure,' said the Legate, and his strange black eyes rested thoughtfully on Marcus. 'No, I am not sure, Aquila.'

'You haven't forgotten my friend, Esca Mac Cunoval, I hope, sir,' Marcus said.

'I remember him very well,' said Claudius with a quick smile to the Briton.

'That ring!' Uncle Aquila suddenly noticed the green stone on Marcus's finger. 'Show it to me.'

'Of course you recognize it?' Marcus said as he gave it to him.

His uncle stood and looked at it for a few moments. 'Yes, I do.' He gave it back. 'How did you come by your father's ring?'

But now was no time to tell the full story. There were slaves on all sides, and Sasticca was getting the dinner ready.

'Uncle Aquila, can I tell you later? It is a long story, and there are many doors to this room.'

Their eyes met.

'Very well,' Uncle Aquila said. 'An hour or two won't make much difference, will it? You agree, Claudius?'

'I certainly do. We will talk in your study after dinner.'

But Marcus was not listening. His hand was running over the young wolf. 'Uncle Aquila, what have you done to Cub? He is nothing but skin and bone.'

'We have done nothing to Cub,' said Uncle Aquila. 'Cub has been breaking his heart for you. Since you left he has refused to eat. He only let that girl Cottia feed him. And now she has gone, he will not eat at all.'

Marcus felt cold suddenly. 'Cottia,' he said. 'Where has Cottia gone?'

'Only to Aquae Sulis for the winter. Her Aunt Valaria wanted to take the waters. They only went a few days ago.'

Marcus began to play with Cub's ears. 'Did she leave any word for me?'

'She came to me in a fine anger, the day before they left, to bring back your ring.'

'Did you take it?'

'I did not. I told her to keep it until she came back in the spring and to give it to you then. "Tell him I shall look after it well all winter" she said.' He smiled at Marcus. 'She is a warm-hearted little thing.'

'Yes,' Marcus said. 'Yes, sir. Now, if we may, Esca and I will take Cub and feed him. Have we time before dinner, Uncle?'

'Plenty of time,' said his uncle. 'Sasticca will want to make a great feast for you, so dinner will be late, I'm sure.'

But Marcus was so tired that he could eat very little of Sasticca's feast. And everything here seemed so different. It was strange to eat at a table after so many meals out of doors. It was strange to wear fine clothes again.

Marcus was glad when at last it was over, and Uncle Aquila said, 'Shall we go up to my study now?'

The two older men moved in that direction, followed by Marcus. But Esca stayed behind. 'I think I won't come,' he said to Marcus.

'Not come? But you must.'

Esca shook his head. 'It is between you and your uncle and the Legate.'

Marcus came back. 'It is between the four of us. What's got into your head, Esca?'

'I don't think I can go into your uncle's study,' Esca said. 'I have been a slave in his house.'

'You are not a slave now.'

'No, I am a free man, now.'

Marcus put his hand on Esca's arm. 'Listen to me. You must put the past behind you. So. You were a slave once. You don't like that. Well, I've got a bad leg. I don't like that. That makes two of us. All we can do about the past is to try to forget it. Come on, Esca. Come up with me now.'

Esca looked up at him with bright eyes. 'I will come,' he said.

The older men were waiting. Outside the windows a gentle rain was falling.

'Well,' said Uncle Aquila at last.

Marcus crossed to the writing-table and set the cloak down

upon it. 'It has lost its wings,' he said. 'That is why it looks so small.'

'So the stories we heard were true,' said the Legate.

'Yes, sir,' Marcus said, and put his hand under the cloak. He turned it back. There stood the lost Eagle: without its wings, but golden and powerful, an Eagle still.

For a long moment nobody spoke. Then Uncle Aquila said, 'Shall we sit down to this?'

Marcus was glad, for his bad leg was beginning to shake under him. Cub lay down over his foot and he began to make his report. He made it clearly and carefully, and at times asked Esca to speak for himself.

The Legate and Uncle Aquila listened closely. No one moved. At last Marcus sat back. There was a silence, then Claudius Hieronimianus spoke. 'You have done well, both of you,' he said. 'Thanks to you, the Painted People will never use the Eagle against our men.'

'And – the Legion?'

'No,' said the Legate. 'I am sorry.'

Marcus knew already, of course. The Ninth Legion could never be formed again, with such a past.

'It is best that it is forgotten,' said the Legate.

'And what about those last few brave men?' Uncle Aquila asked. 'Did they not fight and die for their Legion?'

The Legate turned to look at him. 'A few men cannot make up for the whole Legion,' he said. 'You must see that, Aquila, even if one of them was your brother.'

The Legate turned back to Marcus. 'How many people know that the Eagle has been brought back?'

'South of the Wall, we four and the Commander of the fort at Borcovicus. We told no one else.'

'Good,' said the Legate. 'Of course I shall make a report to Rome. But I know they will decide the same way as I do.'

'And the Eagle?' Uncle Aquila asked.

'We will dig a resting-place for it somewhere,' said the Legate.

'Where?' asked Marcus.

'Why not here in Calleva? Five roads meet here and the

Legions are always passing by.' He bent forward and touched the gold Eagle lightly with one finger. 'So long as Rome lives, the Eagles will pass under the walls of Calleva. What better place for it to lie?'

Very much later that night the four of them stood together, their heads bent down. The Legate stepped forward to the edge of the square hole. The red cloak just showed below in the yellow light; the Eagle lay inside it.

'Here lies the Eagle of the Ninth Legion, the Spanish,' the Legate said. 'It won many great battles. It saw bad times. But at the end it was held high by brave men and true. Now it must be forgotten.'

He stepped back. Esca covered the hole.

Marcus felt tears at the back of his eyes. He was full of sadness for the lost Eagle and the lost Legion.

But I did all I could, he thought. And the Eagle is home again. It will never now be used against its own people. That's something to feel good about, after all.

He lifted his head at the same time as Esca and their eyes met. 'That was good hunting, wasn't it?' Marcus said, with a smile.

19

That winter was not an easy one for Marcus. His leg hurt badly from the months on the run. He felt ill and missed Cottia. The dark winter days seemed to go on for ever.

Then there was the question of his future. What was he to do now?

'Well, I shall stay with you always,' Esca said, when they talked about it. 'From time to time perhaps I shall turn to hunting again, and that will bring in some money.'

Uncle Aquila did not think much of Marcus's idea of becoming a secretary. 'Just you wait a little longer,' he said. 'Wait at least until you're strong again.'

At last spring was in the air. Marcus's leg began to get better. March came and the first leaves grew green on the trees. And quite suddenly the House of Kaeso woke up. For a few days slaves came and went. Then the family returned.

Next morning Marcus went down to the foot of the garden and called for Cottia. It was a wild day of wind, rain and sunshine. Cottia joined him under the fruit-trees.

'I heard you call,' she said, 'so I came. I have brought your ring back to you.'

'Cottia!' Marcus said. 'Well, Cottia!' He stood and looked at her in surprise. She was much taller than a year ago. Her long red-gold hair was now tied up on her head. She looked more than ever like a queen. Her lips were touched with red and there were small gold rings in her ears.

'Well, Cottia, you have grown up,' Marcus said and felt a sense of loss.

'Yes,' said Cottia. 'Do you like me grown up?'

'Yes, yes, of course,' Marcus said. 'Thank you for looking after my ring for me.' He took it from her and put it on. He did not know how to talk to her now. There was a long silence. Then he said with difficulty, 'Did you like Aquae Sulis?'

'No!' Cottia's face was suddenly bright with anger. 'I hated every moment of Aquae Sulis! I never wanted to go there. And all winter I have had no word of you – except one little – *little* message. I have waited, and waited. And now you are not at all glad to see me! Well, I'm not glad to see you, either!'

'You wild little thing!' Marcus caught her arms as she turned to run, and turned her round to face him. Suddenly and softly he laughed. 'But I *am* glad to see you. You do not know how glad I am to see you, Cottia.'

She looked up at him in wonder. 'Yes, you are now,' she said. 'Why weren't you, before?'

'I did not recognize you, just at first.'

'Oh,' said Cottia. Then, 'Where is Cub?'

'Trying to get a bone off Sasticca.'

'All was well with him, then, when you came home?'

85

'He was very thin. He did not eat after you left. But he is all right now.'

'I was afraid of that. That's one of the reasons why I didn't want to go to Aquae Sulis.'

They sat down. After a few moments Cottia asked, 'Did you find the Eagle?'

'Yes,' he answered.

'Oh, Marcus, I am so glad! So very glad! And now?'

'Nothing now.'

'But the Legion?' She searched his face. 'Will there not be a new Ninth Legion after all?'

'No, there will never be a Ninth Legion again.'

'But Marcus,' she began, and then stopped. 'No, I will not ask you questions.'

He smiled. 'One day, maybe, I'll tell you the whole story.'

'I will wait,' said Cottia. 'And what will you do now, Marcus? Will you go back to the Legions?'

Marcus shook his head. 'No, I can never do that. My leg is better but it will never be strong enough.'

'Then what *will* you do?'

'I am not – quite sure.'

'Perhaps you will go home,' she said. There was fear in her eyes. 'You will go back to Rome, and take Cub, and Esca with you?'

'I don't know, Cottia, really I don't. But I don't suppose I shall ever go home.'

But Cottia did not seem to hear him. 'Take me too,' she cried, 'Oh Marcus, take me too!'

'Even to Rome?' he asked.

'Yes,' she said. 'Anywhere at all, if only it is with you.'

Marcus felt happy and sad at once. 'Cottia,' he began, 'Cottia, my heart – it is no use—'

But before he could explain that he had no work and no money, Esca came rushing up. Cub ran behind him.

'This has just come for you,' he said, holding out a paper.

It had the mark of the 6th Legion on it. Uncle Aquila came across the garden to see what it was.

It was from the Legate Claudius Hieronimianus, now in

86

Rome. Marcus read quickly. He looked up. 'Esca, they have made you a free man of Rome – you are a Roman, like me! For what you have done for Rome – and as for me,' he shook his head in surprise, 'they are giving me land and money.'

He stopped reading. He looked round at the faces. 'I can take the land in Britain, or in Etruria, my home.'

My home. He thought of the farm in the warm sun, the flowers and the forests by the sea. Then he looked again at Uncle Aquila, Esca, Cottia.

And he knew that after all Britain was his home now.

'Well done, Marcus,' said Uncle Aquila. 'So you will go back to Etruria soon.'

'It is a new beginning,' Marcus said softly. 'No, uncle, I shall not go back to Etruria. I shall take up my land here in Britain.' He looked at Cottia. 'Not Rome, after all; but you did say "anywhere", didn't you, Cottia my sweet?' he said, and held out his hand to her.

She looked at him for a moment, then smiled, and put her hand in his.

'And now I suppose, I shall have to have a talk with Kaeso,' said Uncle Aquila. 'I don't know, I'm sure. It was so peaceful here before you came.'

Marcus looked out of the window of his uncle's study that evening. Far away, over the miles of forest, he could see the blue hill country. Yes, that's the country for farming, he thought. Esca and I will run our little farm alone. Perhaps we'll pay for some other help from time to time. But we'll manage without slaves.

'We've been talking it over, Esca and I,' he said suddenly, 'and I'm going to try to get land in the Hill Country.'

Uncle Aquila looked up from his writing-table. 'That should not be too difficult,' he said.

'Uncle Aquila, did you know about all this – before, I mean.'

'I knew Claudius was going to do his best for you in Rome. The land's all right, but you'll need more money than they'll give you.'

87

'We'll do well enough, Esca and I. We can do most of the building ourselves, until we grow rich.'

'And Cottia – what will she think of rough huts?'

'Cottia will be happy,' Marcus said.

'Well, you know where to come when you need help.'

'Yes, I know,' Marcus turned from the window. 'If we really need it – after three bad years – I shall come.'

'Not until then?'

'Not until then. No.'

Uncle Aquila shook his head. 'You are impossible! You grow more and more like your father every day!'

'Do I?' Marcus said with a smile. 'Uncle Aquila, you have done so much for me and Esca already. Thank you—'

'Who else have I got to do it for?' Uncle Aquila said roughly. 'I've no son of my own to trouble me. But I'm glad you're not going back to Etruria.' He looked away. 'I might have been quite lonely.'

Yes, that is all behind me now, thought Marcus. My new life is what matters now. My farm, Cottia and Esca.

Somewhere below Esca was singing:

'Oh when I joined the Eagles,
(And it seems like yesterday)
I kissed a girl at Clusium
Before I marched away.'

That's the sound of a free man, Marcus thought, and felt good.

Uncle Aquila looked up again. 'Oh, by the way, I have some news that may interest you. I hear they are building Isca Dumnoniorum again.'

Glossary

(The glossary gives the meaning of the word as it is used in this book. Other possible meanings are not given.)

arrow a stick with a pointed end used as a weapon

centurion the leader of a hundred men in the Roman army

chariot a car with two wheels used for fighting and racing: a charioteer is a man who drives a chariot

cloak a type of coat with no arm-holes; it is tied at the neck only

cohort there were ten cohorts in a legion

cover a hiding-place during a hunt; to **break cover** is to come out from the hiding-place

druid a type of priest among the people of Gaul, Britain, and Ireland

eagle a large bird; the sign of the Roman legions. It was believed to give the Roman soldiers luck and power

fortress a strong building which soldiers live in and guard; it is built to stop attacks

gate an entrance, or a door with metal bars

gladiator a slave who has to fight to the death in a Roman theatre

holy something which belongs to the gods, or is believed to be close to gods

hut a small wooden building

legate the commander of a legion

legion a part of the Roman army; a legion has between 3,000 and 6,000 men

master a slave-owner

prefect a Roman official

Roman of Rome – the capital city of Italy

slave a person who is owned and forced to work by another person

spear a long weapon with a metal point

standard a long stick on which the Eagle is fixed; it is carried into battle at the head of the soldiers

torch a piece of burning wood used to give light

tribe a group of people who speak the same language and usually have one head-man

Wall Hadrian's Wall – a wall with fortresses, in a line across Britain, between England and Scotland

wolf a wild animal which looks like a dog

Alpha Books

Alpha Books is an exciting new series of readers for the student of English. Novels by well-known authors have been selected for adaptation on the strength of their plot and the quality of the writing. Each adapted version closely follows the story of the original, and retains as much as possible of the book's atmosphere and style. Careful control of the language and vocabulary provides a clear and straightforward text which allows the student to enjoy reading without constantly having to reach for the dictionary.

The Alpha series includes classics, crime, science-fiction, romances, historical fiction, thrillers, westerns, general fiction, and non-fiction, and provides a wide collection of English reading to meet all interests and tastes.

Some current and forthcoming titles are:

For a complete list of published titles and more information, please write to: ELT Marketing, Oxford University Press, Walton Street, Oxford, OX2 6DP

Alpha Historical Fiction

Rosemary Sutcliff
Outcast

Sickness and death came to the tribe. They said it was because of Beric. They said he had brought down the Anger of the Gods. The warriors of the tribe cast him out. Alone without friends, family, or tribe, Beric faced the dangers of the Roman world.

This is a fast-moving story of adventure, set against a background of slave markets, thieves, and the horror of the Roman galleys.

Harold Keith
Comanche

'I have heard the Bells of Death, and I am still alive.'

The Comanches murdered his mother, took away his young brother, and made him their prisoner. Now Pedro Pavon lived the life of the Comanches – a life where only the strong stay alive and the weak are left to die. The squaws laughed at him, and the warriors whipped him like a dog. But he grew hard like the Comanches and became a man.

He learnt how to ride like an Indian, hunt buffaloes like an Indian. He rode on their war parties and danced the Battle Dance. And he fell in love with Willow Girl who was married to another man. For her sake he travelled across the wildest, hottest parts of the South-West in search of the beautiful horses of Tafoya.

Geoffrey Household
Rogue Male

'Nothing could hurt me. I lived only in the present.
The future was black, but I didn't think of the future.
I was just a hunted animal – resting.'

It was a war – one man against a nation. He wanted
no help. He needed no friends. Their agents hunted him
like a wild animal.

Rogue Male is a classic thriller – a breathtaking manhunt
across pre-war Europe – murder a hundred feet below
the streets of London – and in a quiet corner of England
the hunt to the death.

Lionel Davidson

The Rose of Tibet

Houston came back from Tibet with a story that was hard to believe. But he did not tell it. He lay alone in a London hospital where they cut off his right arm. They gave him something for the pain. It helped him not to worry about his half million pounds. But other people did. Many other people.

This is Houston's story – a story of the high mountains and the man who came from beyond the sunset. A story of love and death and the strange and beautiful girl they called the Rose of Tibet.